THE

TEXAS

BROTHERHOOD

Home to Texas and straight to the altar!

A home. A family. A legacy of their own.

Mustang Valley has long been home to the brotherhood. United by blood, trust and loyalty, these men fight for what they believe—for family, for what's right and ultimately…for love.

Now there are newcomers in their midst. Two gorgeous new Randell brothers are back to reclaim their heritage, find their family and just maybe discover the women of their dreams….

Dear Reader,

I'm so pleased that I have the opportunity to return to Mustang Valley and revisit the Randell men from my TEXAS BROTHERHOOD series. You will want to find out what Jack Randell's boys, Chance, Cade and Travis, have been up to. Along with their half brothers Jared Trager and Wyatt and Dylan Gentry, they have all adjusted to the valley. I'm here to say that they're all doing well, including Hank Barrett, the adopted patriarch of the family.

My inspiration for this series and Hank's character was my dear friend Hence Barrow, a West Texas rancher. He's the one who taught this city girl all about ranching. You see, his family had been doing it for over a hundred years. I'm sorry to say that Hence passed away this past year at the age of ninety-seven, but I'll never forget his stories and his love of the land. It was an honor and privilege to know him, and to be called his friend. I'll miss you, Hence.

In this series, I bring Jack's brother Sam Randell's sons, Luke and Brady, to the valley. In the first story, Luke—the real estate tycoon—wants to take his estranged father's inheritance and sell his share of the Rocking R. It's the Randell cousins who step in and teach him about family and tradition. His pretty blond ranch foreman, Tess Meyers, teaches him to love. And one little five-year-old girl steals his heart.

There are many more surprises. Hope you enjoy it.

With regards,

Patricia Thayer

PATRICIA THAYER
Luke: The Cowboy Heir

TORONTO NEW YORK LONDON
AMSTERDAM PARIS SYDNEY HAMBURG
STOCKHOLM ATHENS TOKYO MILAN MADRID
PRAGUE WARSAW BUDAPEST AUCKLAND

Recycling programs
for this product may
not exist in your area.

ISBN-13: 978-0-373-36531-9

LUKE: THE COWBOY HEIR

First published in the U.K. under the title
THE BLACK SHEEP'S PROPOSAL.

First North American Publication 2009.

Copyright © 2008 by Patricia Wright

www.Harlequin.com

Printed in U.S.A.

Patricia Thayer has been writing for over twenty years, and has published thirty novels with Harlequin® Books. Her books have been nominated for various awards in the U.S.A. including the National Readers' Choice Award, the Book Buyers' Best and a prestigious RITA® Award. In 1997, *Nothing Short of a Miracle* won the *Romantic Times BOOKreviews* Reviewers' Choice Award for Best Special Edition.

Thanks to the understanding men in her life— her husband of over thirty-five years, Steve, and her three grown sons and three grandsons—Pat has been able to fulfill her dream of writing. Besides writing romance, she loves to travel— especially in the West, where she researches her books firsthand. You might find her on a ranch in Texas, or on a train to an old mining town in Colorado or on an adventure in Scotland. Just so long as she can share it all with her favorite hero, Steve. She loves to hear from readers. You can write to her at P.O. Box 6251, Anaheim, CA 92816-0251, U.S.A., or check her Web site at www.patriciathayer.com for upcoming books.

To Hence,

Thank you for sharing your life, the wonderful stories and your family. I'll miss you, friend.

1909–2007

CHAPTER ONE

HE'D sworn he would never come back here.

Luke Randell hadn't been left with a choice. He released a long breath and climbed out of his BMW. His gaze swept the area that had once been his childhood home. The Rocking R Ranch.

Large oak trees shaded the green lawn. A concrete walkway led to the wraparound porch of the big, well-kept Victorian house. A recent coat of white paint covered the two-story house where he used to live, more than twenty-seven years ago. A rush of feelings—sadness and a lot of bitterness—hit him as he glanced toward the large barn, outbuildings and corral. They, too, had been well cared for.

Not what he'd expected when he'd left Dallas to return to San Angelo, Texas. A warm breeze brushed against his face, and he caught a whiff of the ranch's earthy smells, causing a flood of more memories—memories of his pony, Jazzy, then his horse, Bandit, the chestnut gelding he'd been given for his fifth birthday.

Damn. He'd loved that horse.

Tightness gripped Luke's chest as he thought about the

painful day his daddy had sold the animal…. That same day everything had changed. No more perfect family. For a six-year-old kid it had been the end of the world.

He quickly shook off the foolish sentiment and walked along the path to the porch, then up the steps. His gaze caught the wrought-iron branding symbol of the Rocking R nailed next to the door.

Another memory hit him before he could push it away. He couldn't keep doing this. Not if he was going to live here in his childhood home. The heavy oak door had been opened inward, leaving a wood-framed screen door to keep out intruders. He shrugged. It was the country, not downtown Dallas.

"Hello… Anyone here?" he called.

He waited for an answer. When none came, he walked inside the large entry hall. The hardwood floors were polished, showing off their honey color. The front parlor, as his mother used to call it, also sparkled with polish and a lemony scent. There were several antiques, but the dark brocade sofa and chairs still looked uncomfortable.

Who cares? he asked himself. With any luck, he wouldn't be here that long. Right now he needed to find Ray Meyers. Suddenly a sound interrupted his thoughts. On the open staircase that led to the second floor he found a black kitten with white paws.

"Well, at least someone's here to welcome me."

He got another meow as he walked over and picked up the kitten. "Maybe you can tell me where everyone is."

The cat meowed again just as muffled voices came from upstairs. "Looks like I got my answer." He started up the steps, carrying his new companion. He walked along the hall past several rooms, one of which used to be his. He ignored it. No sense stirring up more memories.

Luke continued on toward the open door to the master bedroom. Once across the threshold, he found the source of the voices. He leaned against the doorway and enjoyed the view.

A woman was on her hands and knees with her head buried under the large four-poster bed. He couldn't help but notice how well she filled out her fitted jeans. Next to her was a little girl not more than four or five.

"Mommy, we have to find Jinx. She gets scared when she's all alone." The child's long, blond hair was pulled back into a ponytail. Her worried look didn't take away from her cute features. Just then the woman's head appeared, and Luke's heart shot off racing. The little girl definitely got her good looks from her mother.

Her wheat-colored hair was pulled back in a ponytail, also, and was a shade darker than the child's. Her profile was near perfect, along with her creamy complexion. He cursed silently for noticing, and cursed again for wanting to see more.

"Excuse me," he said.

The two females swung around toward him. Okay, both mother and daughter were gorgeous. Somehow he managed to find his voice. "Could this little guy be who you're looking for?"

"Jinx!" The small child jumped up and ran to him. "You found my kitty."

Luke handed the furry bundle to her. "I think it found me." He brushed his hands off and glanced at the woman.

Tess didn't like being caught off guard. Over the last several months her entire life had been turned upside down, and she suspected this stranger was the big reason.

He walked toward her and extended a hand. "Luke Randell."

She climbed to her feet. "Tess Meyers." She shook his hand. It was not rough like a rancher's, but his grip was strong.

"This is my daughter, Olivia."

Her daughter looked at Mr. Randell. "But everybody calls me Livy, and this is Jinx."

"Well, hello, Livy…and Jinx."

Tess drew his attention back to her. "We weren't expecting you for a few more days, Mr. Randell."

"My plans changed." His gaze bore into hers. "Is there a problem?"

"None whatsoever," she lied. "I just wanted to make sure the house was ready for you." No way was she ready for this man with his dark good looks and silver eyes. Just what San Angelo needed. Another handsome Randell man.

He glanced around. "I didn't expect any of this, but I appreciate it. Thank you."

"Outside of needing linens on the bed, the house should be livable."

He nodded toward the fresh sheets on the bare mattress. "I think I can manage to make up a bed."

She nodded. No doubt he could mess up a bed, too.

She groaned. Where had that come from? "Oh, I plugged in the refrigerator, but I'm afraid there isn't any food in the house."

"Not a problem. I stopped by the grocery store and bought some staples."

She couldn't help but stare at the man dressed in his knife-pressed jeans, navy polo shirt and topsider shoes looking like the last person anyone would expect to take over a cattle ranch—a ranch she and her father had put a lot of work into, which, there was a good possibility, could be taken away from them. She had to be very careful. This man held her future in his hands.

"Okay then, I guess we'll be going and let you get settled in." She started for the door. "Come on, Livy."

"But, Mom, I didn't ask him yet." She stood rooted in the middle of the room, gripping her kitty. "Do you have any little girls I can play with?"

The new owner looked surprised by the question, but finally he said, "No, sorry, I don't."

"Oh…" Livy looked disappointed. "That's the reason I got a kitty because I don't have anyone to play with." She held up Jinx. "Mommy said she wasn't going to have any more babies…and I got him so I won't get lonely."

"Olivia Meyers," Tess said, mortified. "It's time we let Mr. Randell move in."

"Okay." Her daughter complied and walked to her mother. "Goodbye, Mr. Randell."

"Goodbye, Livy…Jinx." He looked at Tess. "Mrs. Meyers."

"It's Miss Meyers." She didn't know why she corrected him. "Ray Meyers is my father, not my husband."

Livy chimed in once again. "Yeah... Mommy doesn't have a husband, and I don't have a daddy."

Thirty minutes later, Tess sat at the kitchen table in the foreman's cottage.

"I was mortified, Bernice," Tess said.

Her aunt shook her head. "The child sure has a mind of her own." She carried their lunch plates to the sink. "Now, tell me, is Luke Randell as handsome as his cousins?"

Bernice was her dad's younger sister. In her late fifties, she'd lost her husband a few years ago. When Ray Meyers first took ill last year, Bernice didn't hesitate to come and help out.

Tess shrugged. "If you like the preppy look. He's definitely not a rancher. I doubt he's capable or has any desire to run this place."

"He could learn," Bernice told her. "My goodness, he has six cousins who do some sort of ranching. It's in his blood."

"What if he doesn't want to ranch, but instead sells the Rocking R?"

Those soft hazel eyes met hers. "Doesn't he have to wait for his brother to show up before he could do anything?"

She nodded. "They do own it jointly."

She'd been notified of Sam Randell's death by the lawyer, who also let them know that the ranch had been left to his two sons, Luke and Brady.

"Maybe Brady Randell wants to sell, too. He's a pilot in the air force. Why would he want a ranch?"

With a shrug, Bernice filled the sink and added

some liquid soap. Tess picked up a towel to dry. "And maybe those boys will decide to continue to lease the Rocking R to you."

"Sam Randell leased the land to Ray Meyers. And we both know Dad can't run this place any longer."

Sadness crept in as Tess leaned against the counter in the small kitchen. She'd grown up in this house. Back then it had been just her and her dad. Now it was pretty crowded with Bernice and Livy added into the mix.

That's why Tess had moved into her daughter's bedroom. It was more convenient for everyone to have Bernice move into Tess's room.

She knew this setup was only temporary. His disease was progressing, and his good days were becoming fewer. He hardly ever left his room. It made her sad to think of her father's mind slowly erasing memories of his life…and that he was not always able to remember his daughter, or his granddaughter.

Tess shook away the sad thoughts. "I need to talk to Mr. Randell. I need to know what he's going to do, so I can make some plans." She was hopeful she could stay on and continue to lease this house, along with barn space for the horses. She needed to make a living for her family. And there was her father's cattle operation. Although small, she didn't want to sell the calves yet. Roundup wasn't for another few months.

But if the worst happened and they had to leave, she'd get another place. She doubted she could find as good a setup as the Rocking R Ranch. Her father had built several of the horse stalls in the barn. The large corral had been Ray's handiwork, too. That had been the reason the lease agreement was so cheap; her dad had also been the caretaker.

They'd had such big plans as partners. The Meyerses were going to breed and train quarter horses. And her bay stallion, Smooth Whiskey Doc, was going to be their cutting champion. So far she had made something of a name as a trainer and rider. But she wanted and needed the money that her future champion stallion could bring in. She wasn't thinking about herself, but Olivia. She was her sole parent.

Her aunt's voice brought her back. "What?"

"Go work Whiskey," Bernice said. "That always calms you."

She shook her head. "Dad will be up from his nap soon."

"Go. I can look after Ray." She turned her niece around and nudged her toward the door. "Take a break, Tess. You need it."

Tess didn't argue, just headed for the door. She found Livy on the porch playing with her dolls and the kitten.

"Hey, sweetie, I want you to stay on the porch. It's too hot to go out in the sun."

"Mommy, can I go see Grandpa? I'll be quiet. I promise."

It was so sad. Livy and her grandpa Ray had had a close relationship since the day she was born. Now most of the time he couldn't speak to her. "I think he'd like that. But maybe you should leave Jinx in the box in our room."

"I will, Mommy. I know Grandpa doesn't mean to, but he sometimes squeezes too hard."

She knelt down in front of her daughter. "You know Grandpa's sick. He doesn't mean to squeeze too hard."

Livy's blond ponytail bobbed up and down. "I know, Mommy. I wish he wasn't sick."

"So do I, sweetie." Tess had to fight her tears. "You're my best girl."

Livy smiled. "And you're my bestest mom."

They exchanged a kiss and then Tess started off, but her daughter called to her. "Are you going to go see Mr. Randell?"

"No, honey, Mr. Randell is busy. I'm going to work with Whiskey."

Livy's eyes narrowed. Tess knew her daughter was cooking up something else. "He's a nice man. Maybe we should bake him a cake to welcome him home."

Butter up the enemy. That was an idea. "We'll talk about it later. Remember, don't leave the porch." She turned and walked toward the barn, knowing that ploy wasn't going to work for long. She had to come up with something to keep Livy from intruding on Luke Randell.

Putting her wide-brimmed cowboy hat on her head, she glanced toward the large Victorian house. Perched on a hill with a grove of pecan trees lined up on either side for shade and protection from the elements, it was a sight to behold.

She'd heard stories that Mrs. Sam Randell had been so humiliated when her husband's brother, Jack, had been sent to prison for cattle rustling, she insisted they leave the area. It had been twenty-seven years since anyone had lived there.

"Your father did a wonderful job with the upkeep," a man's voice said.

Tess swung around to find Luke Randell. "Oh, Mr. Randell…"

"Please, call me Luke."

"Luke, and I'm Tess," she said, a little breathless.

He'd changed into a long-sleeved shirt and a pair of boots. Cocked on his head was a worn cowboy hat, giving him a rugged look.

"Do I fit in a little better?"

Tess was tall at five-nine, but had to look up at him. Stand back was more like it. "You fit in dressed like you were before, but this is more practical for the ranch."

"Especially if I'm headed for the barn." He smiled, and it caused her pulse to race. Great. She was acting like a teenager.

"You want to see the barn?"

He glanced around. "Actually, I was looking for your father. Is he around?"

Oh, no. She wasn't ready to discuss her father's… situation yet. "I'm sorry, but he isn't feeling well right now." She rushed on to say, "I'm sure I can answer anything you want to know."

"I just wanted to let him…and you—know that my arriving early isn't meant to disturb your operation. You still have another two months on your lease. As the lawyer informed you, I'm just living in the house until a decision is made about the property."

A decision? "What about your brother?"

Luke still had trouble getting used to that term…for Brady. "Half brother," he clarified. "Brady is a pilot in the air force, and the only information I've gotten from the military so far is that he's overseas. I left word for him to contact me here."

"So your plans are to sell the ranch?"

Luke sighed. If only he could, it sure would solve his immediate problems. "There are a lot of things to consider when or if this place goes on the market." His gaze locked with her rich blue eyes and it caused him to get temporarily distracted. He quickly glanced away. He wasn't about to let that happen…again.

"I know you and your father need more information than that," he told her. "But it's all I can give for now."

She nodded. "Of course, Dad and I would love to continue the lease arrangement we have now." She gave him a sideways glance as they started walking toward the barn. "Are you considering staying on…and running the ranch?"

He frowned. "Technically I've never ranched before. I was just a kid when we moved away."

"But you still have a lot of family here. I'm sure they'd help out."

They came to the barn and he slid open the large door. "So you know the Randells?"

Tess nodded. "There's something else. The lease arrangement your father had with my father could continue…or if you'd like to raise cattle under your own brand, we could stay on as the foreman." She shrugged. "It's just something to think about."

Not waiting for an answer, Tess walked into the cool interior. Although the barn was clean and well organized, the smell of hay and horses was prevalent, and she liked the earthy scent. She headed down the concrete

aisle, passing several empty stalls. She was hoping to
have them filled by now, but without her father's help
she couldn't board any more horses.

There were two quarter horses here she'd been
working with, but her main focus was still on Whiskey.
Taking the time, she greeted the valuable equines before
she reached the last stall. Her bay stallion greeted her
with a soft whinny, and he nuzzled her hand.

"How's my favorite guy?" she crooned. "You ready
to work?" He bobbed his head.

"This is Smooth Whiskey Doc. He's the future
cutting champion."

With an ease that surprised Tess, Luke walked up to
Whiskey and stroked him. "Hey, fella, how you doing?"
Whiskey took to the attention and moved closer to the
stranger. "You sure are a beauty."

"Don't give him too much praise. It'll just go to his
head."

"So you breed horses?"

She nodded. "Been working on it. I've had a lot of
help from Chance Randell. He also breeds quarter
horses. I've done some training and competing with my
mare, Lady. I helped out Chance with training, in trade
for his stallion, Whiskey Pete, to breed with my mare,
and as a result we got Smooth Whiskey Doc."

"You're partners?"

She couldn't help but laugh. "Hardly. Chance doesn't
need me. He's made quite a name for himself on his
own. He just did me a favor." She patted the horse's
neck. "And I appreciate it. As neighbors we all kind of
help each other out."

"So you and your father aren't running cattle any longer?"

"There's just a small herd now."

Here was her opportunity. "Cattle isn't our main focus anymore. Like I said, we've been breeding and training cutting horses for competition. And if for any reason, you and your bother decide to stay, I'd—we'd like to continue to rent the foreman's cottage and rent barn space to board the horses."

Luke Randell just stood there for a long time, then finally spoke. "I can't say one way or the other what will happen now. I have no plans to ranch at this time. To be honest, I never planned to come back here…ever. So as soon as it's possible for me, I'll be leaving."

Tess was angry. "And the hell with us."

He blinked at her bluntness. "You have two months to relocate."

The man didn't have a heart. "The Rocking R has been my father's and my home for well over twenty years. My daughter hasn't lived anywhere else." She hated that she sounded so desperate. But she was. "It isn't so easy to move a family and livestock." Or a father who barely remembers his name, she added silently. She studied the stubborn look on his face. "Besides, how can you be so anxious to sell land that's been in your family for generations?"

Luke Randell stiffened, then glanced away, but not before she saw a flash of emotion. "Maybe because that family deserted me a long time ago."

CHAPTER TWO

AN HOUR later, Luke leaned against a post on the back porch. He held a long-neck bottle in his hand as he watched Tess Meyers work her quarter horse in the corral.

Impressive. He took a thirsty drink of beer. She looked strong astride the powerful stallion, and the two together were as graceful as a ballet, moving in perfect unison in their performance.

There were a half-dozen steers in the pen, and she and Whiskey easily separated a calf from the others, then drove it back into the herd. Even from a distance, he caught her smile as she patted the horse's neck affectionately after he completed his task.

Once again his body stirred. For the second time in hours this cowgirl had him wondering about things he had no business thinking about.

Luke sat on the porch swing and propped his booted feet on the railing. What the hell was he doing here? He never wanted to come back to this place. The home he'd once loved, where he'd been part of a family. That had ended when his parents divorced, his dad went back into the military and his mother took him to live in Dallas.

He closed his eyes and he could still hear the fights late at night. Doors slamming, his dad starting the car and driving off. The worst sound was of his mother's crying. He hated his father for that. Most of all he hated Sam Randell for deserting them.

Now, all these years later, he had no choice but to come back here. The perfect scenario would be to sell the place, make some money and start over.

He doubted he could go back to Dallas. Thanks to a bad deal, his reputation had been destroyed in the real estate business. Because of a woman, Gina Chilton, he'd gotten involved with the wrong people. Her daddy, Buck Chilton, had invested money in his real estate venture.

In the end Luke had barely escaped criminal charges, and it had cost him everything. His employees hadn't fared much better, but at least he'd been able to give them a severance package. That meant there'd been nothing left for him. Everything he'd worked so hard to build was all gone now. Just some personal things, his clothes and the car remained. And he had to sell the luxury vehicle so he'd have some money to live on.

Well, at least he had a roof over his head…for now.

"Hey, mister. Are you sleeping?" a young voice said.

Luke opened his eyes and saw little Livy Meyers standing on the porch step. She was wearing jeans and a ruffled pink blouse, holding her kitten.

He dropped his feet on the floor. "No, just doing some thinking." He glanced around to see if Tess Meyers was around. "Does your mother know where you are?"

Looking sheepish, the child moved to the top step.

"Kinda." She shrugged. "She said not to bother you 'cause you were moving in. Are you finished?"

With what was left of his furniture in storage, he had only a few suitcases to empty. "Yes, I'm moved in."

She smiled at him, and something tightened in his chest. She strolled to the swing and sat down. "I'm glad. And I'm glad you came here to live, too. You want to hold Jinx again? He likes you."

"You think so, huh?" He couldn't help but take her offering. He doubted many people could resist her big blue eyes and dimples. The kitten immediately curled up against his chest and closed his eyes.

"Hey, mister, see he likes you." She studied him. "So do I."

"Well, I like you, too. Maybe you could call me Luke."

She frowned. "Mama says I can't call big people by their first names 'cause it's not 'spectful."

"Respectful," Luke corrected gently.

She nodded. "Yeah. Maybe I can call you Mr. Luke."

Luke wasn't used to being around kids. But Livy Meyers didn't seem to notice. "Sounds like a good idea."

Her smile widened, and he saw the resemblance to her pretty mother. But the smile suddenly disappeared when someone called Livy's name.

They both turned to see Tess coming out of the corral. "Oh, no. I gotta go." She grabbed her kitten and went to the edge of the porch. "I forgot to ask you something." She came back. "What's your favorite flavor of cake?"

He blinked. "I guess it would be chocolate. Why?"

Livy leaned forward and whispered, "It's a surprise." Giggling, the little nymph ran off toward her mother.

Tess approached her daughter, and he didn't have to hear to know that the child was getting a lecture. With a nod, Livy started for the foreman's house while Tess headed his way.

Luke stood, feeling a little rush of excitement on seeing her graceful strides, and those long legs encased in jeans and covered with worn leather chaps. She wore a Henley-style shirt and her battered cowboy hat on her head. Suddenly he couldn't remember why he swore off women. He adjusted his own hat and went to meet her.

"I want to apologize for Livy bothering you," Tess began. "It won't happen again."

"She wasn't a bother. She asked if I was busy. So please don't let her think I'm some sort of ogre." Why did he care what a five-year-old thought?

"Well, she still shouldn't have come here. I told her to stay on the porch."

"Technically she was on the porch."

Tess jammed her hands on her hips and frowned. "Not her porch. And with you living here now, she especially needs to know boundaries. There are too many things that could happen to her around a ranch."

"I understand." He nodded. "But there's also no reason for us to avoid one another."

"Of course." She sighed. "I'm sorry, Mr. Randell—"

"Please, it's Luke."

Tess hesitated. She didn't want to get too friendly with this man. "Luke… It's just that there's never been anyone living in the house."

"Like I said, it's temporary. And I don't want or plan to disturb your operation."

"So you aren't giving any more thought to staying and going into ranching?"

Not in the last hour. "I've never given any thought to staying permanently," he said stubbornly.

Tess couldn't understand how he could walk away from this incredible property. "Maybe you should talk to your cousins before you make a decision."

He arched an eyebrow. "Oh, yeah, the notorious Randell brothers."

She didn't miss the resentment in his voice. "Your family runs several successful businesses. There's the guest ranch…along with horse breeding and a cattle operation. Not to mention being a supplier of rough rodeo stock."

"Don't forget my uncle who was arrested for cattle rustling and cousins who were juvenile delinquents. My uncle and my daddy were well-known womanizers."

Tess tried not to react, but it was hard. "Those are old stories. Chance, Cade and Travis have all but erased that bad reputation with their work in the community. You should give San Angelo a chance."

He blew out a long breath. "That still doesn't make me a rancher."

Here was her chance. "But I am. I could run this place for you."

He stared at her for a long time. "You're asking to be my foreman?"

She fought the blush coloring her cheeks. "It's not as crazy as it sounds. I've worked alongside my daddy as soon as I could climb on a horse. I was three years old when we first came here."

Tess recalled her father's stories about how he'd used her mother's life insurance money to buy the first herd. She thought about her father now and she grew sad, knowing he was going to have to leave here, anyway.

Luke's gray eyes filled with mischief. "So you think you can make a rancher out of me?"

Her pulse raced as she looked him over. "You are a Randell, so I'd say it's already been bred into you."

Two mornings later Luke was still thinking about Tess Meyers. She'd managed to interrupt his thoughts sporadically in the past forty-eight hours. Although he'd spent most of the time in solitude, and his meals had consisted of frozen dinners he put into the small microwave he'd brought with him, he still wanted to eat in peace. The crazy thing was, he actually had thought about her offer…all of thirty seconds.

Luke sipped his coffee and leaned against the kitchen counter. The room was huge with built-in cupboards that lined the walls. The countertops were a golden-hued Mexican tile, and the floor was covered in terra-cotta brick.

He smiled. He remembered it vividly since he used to eat breakfast here as a child. The very same table was placed by the row of windows that overlooked the barn and corral. Back then there were ranch hands around, helping his father run the place. Sam had gotten out of the military…and he was finally home with his family.

Luke had just turned five and gotten a new horse for his birthday that summer. He rode Bandit every day until he went off to kindergarten. Life could have been better, but it could get a lot worse. Parents could fight and decide to end a marriage…destroy a family. And a boy might never see his dad again.

Luke shook away the thoughts. Damn. Stop it. He was an adult now. He'd gotten over all that long ago. He'd moved on. Or had he?

There was a knock on the door, pulling him back to the present. He looked through the screen and saw Livy and an older woman.

Surprisingly he was happy to see her. "Morning, shortcake. You came back."

"It's okay, I'm 'posed to be here now."

"I'm glad." He opened the door. "Who's your friend?"

Livy giggled. "She's not my friend, she's my aunt Bernie."

"Bernice Peterson," the older woman said, and offered a warm smile that crinkled the corners of her hazel eyes. "Please call me Bernice."

"Nice to meet you, Bernice. I'm Luke. Would you come in?"

Both females walked into the kitchen. "I hope it's not too early, but I wanted to bring you some biscuits while they were still warm from the oven."

"Of course it's never too early if you bring food," he said. "You must have heard my stomach growling all the way to your house." He took the basket, placed it on the counter and dug out a soft, steaming biscuit. He took a bite and groaned. "Delicious. I could get used to this."

"Thank you." She grinned. "I do appreciate a man with an appetite."

"And I appreciate home cooking. Would you like some coffee?"

"No, thank you. We need to get back to the house."

"Yeah, we can't leave Grandpa by himself," Livy told him. "And Mommy's in the corral working Whiskey. He's gonna be the NCHA champion some day," she announced proudly.

"Olivia, it's not nice to brag," Bernice said. "Now, ask Mr. Luke before we wear out our welcome."

"My mom, Aunt Bernie and me want to invite you to supper tomorrow night." The child's eyes widened. "Will you come? Aunt Bernie is making our favorite, pot roast with those tiny potatoes. And there'll be a surprise…"

This child was a charmer. So different from her mother's no-nonsense attitude. "Well, how can I turn down an invitation like that? I'd love to come. What time?"

"Say six o'clock," Bernice said as she started for the door. "Come on, Livy, we need to get back to Grandpa."

"I hope Mr. Meyers feels better soon."

Livy looked up at him, her eyes sad. "Grandpa is really sick. He doesn't even read me stories anymore." Her gaze widened. "Do you read stories, Mr. Luke?"

Tess stood in her father's bedroom. "It's okay, Dad. I can do it for you."

"No," Ray Meyers argued, pushing her hand away. "I can button my own damn shirt."

Tess stood back, but watched protectively as her aging father worked at the simple task. Today was one of his more lucid days. And she was grateful.

His fingers were clumsy but he managed the job.

The sixty-five-year-old one-time rodeo cowboy, horse trainer and rancher looked used up. She brushed a tear from her eye. His thinning hair was more white than gray. His lined skin was liver spotted and his blue eyes were tired…and sad. To her he was the most wonderful man in the world. And soon he wouldn't remember her…or his granddaughter.

"Hey, Dad, you want to sit outside today? It's not too hot yet."

"I don't want to sit on the porch…I need to check the herd." He glanced at Tess and a strange look came over him. "Mary Theresa, why aren't you in school?" he asked, suddenly agitated "You don't want me to get into trouble again do you?"

"No, Daddy. I don't." She knelt down next to his chair. "You know I love going on roundups with you." She wanted to store up all the memories she could, no matter if they were decades old.

"And I love you with me, too, baby girl. But you need to go to school." He brushed his hand over her head and cupped her cheeks. "You're so pretty…just like your mama."

A tear ran down her face. "I love you, Daddy."

"I love you, too." Then the look in eyes changed to confusion and Tess knew she'd lost him.

"How about if I turn on the television and you can watch *The Price is Right*?" She didn't wait for an answer as she pressed the remote to the game show, then left the room.

Bernice looked up from her crossword puzzle at the kitchen, but Tess didn't want to talk right now. She needed an escape for a few hours. She turned to Livy who was playing with her cat on the back porch.

"Hey, sweetie, how would you like to go riding?"

It was late morning, and the August sun was beginning to heat up by the time Tess saddled the horses. Her dad's gelding, Dusty, was ready for Livy. The old buckskin hadn't been ridden much lately, and the exercise would be good for him. She led Whiskey and Dusty out of the barn. That's when she looked up and saw Luke pull his car up at the back of the house and get out.

"Mom, look it's Mr. Luke." Before she could stop her daughter, the child took off running. "Hi, Mr. Luke," she called.

"Hey, shortcake," he called back and started toward the corral. He was in a pair of faded jeans and a chambray shirt and boots. He sure didn't look like a businessman.

Tess watched her daughter beam as she approached him. "We're going riding."

"Seems like a nice day for it," he said as he caught up to the child. His gaze met Tess's and offered an easy smile.

Ignoring the funny tingle, she touched her finger to her hat and nodded. "C'mon, Livy. We need to get going."

The child seemed hesitant, then said, "Mommy, can Mr. Luke go with us?" She turned back to the man in question. "You can ride Dusty…he's real gentle."

It wasn't a good idea. "Livy, Mr. Luke probably has a lot of things to do today."

The girl looked up at her new hero. "Do you?"

Luke slipped his hands into his pockets. He wasn't

sure what to do. He didn't want to sit around the house all day…again. He shrugged, but felt his excitement grow. "No. I'm free. I wouldn't mind seeing a little of the ranch."

The child grinned. "See, Mommy. He wants to see the ranch."

He watched Tess struggle with her decision. He couldn't blame her, he was a threat to her family's future.

She finally said. "Okay, you can ride Dusty, and, Livy, you'll have to double up with me."

Livy jumped up and down. "Oh, boy." She grabbed Luke's hand and nearly pulled him to the corral.

Tess tied the reins to the railing. "You'll need to adjust the stirrups."

"I think I remember how."

He went to work as she boosted Livy up on Whiskey. Then she went around to the other side of Dusty and helped him with his task. Finished with the one stirrup, Luke came around to the other side. Standing next to her, he caught the soft scent of soap and shampoo. He stole a quick glance at her face to find her skin scrubbed clean of any makeup, revealing a dash of freckles across her nose. She looked like a teenager.

"That should do it." She squinted up at him. "Just give Dusty his lead, and he'll do the rest."

Luke nodded, happy to have something else to concentrate on. He jammed his boot into the stirrup, grabbed the horn and boosted himself onto the horse.

Excitement went through Luke as he walked the buckskin away from the corral gate and tested some basic commands.

"How does it feel?" Tess asked.

"Good." He glanced at her and smiled. "Real good."

"Okay, let's go," Livy said.

"Hold your horses," Tess said as she climbed up behind her daughter.

The child giggled. "That's funny, Mommy."

Luke couldn't take his eyes off Tess. She easily handled the stallion. The animal danced away, but she got him under control with expert hands and soothing voice.

They started off toward the south. Once in the open meadow, Livy turned to her mother. "I want to go faster, Mommy," the child urged her.

Tess smiled. "You do, do you? How fast?"

"Really, really fast."

She gave a sideways glance at Luke. "We'll be right back." She made a clicking sound with her mouth as she squeezed the horse's sides. Whiskey shot off in a run, then gradually began circling the pasture.

Luke didn't like being left behind, and neither did Dusty. "What do you think, boy? Should we try to catch them?"

The horse bobbed his head. The instant Luke touched the heel of his boot against the animal, he took off. Awkward at first, Luke soon found the rhythm as he followed the female duo.

Tess spotted Luke coming toward them. He didn't look bad on a horse and more than capable of handling Dusty. She also couldn't help but notice his broad shoulders and taut body. So the hotshot businessman was playing cowboy.

She pulled on the reins to slow Whiskey so the other horse and rider could catch up.

"Mommy, let's show Mr. Luke the ponies."

"The mustangs? They still around here?" Luke asked, pulling up beside them.

Tess nodded. "They are." It wouldn't hurt to show him what he was giving up. "Are you up for the ride?"

"Sure."

About fifteen minutes later, they reached the edge of the Rocking R property, a large section of land called Mustang Valley. There were three other ranches that bordered this area, too. She slowed her horse, and Luke rode up next to them.

"You did pretty well," she told him, and patted Dusty's neck. "And this guy sure needed the exercise."

Luke pulled off his hat and wiped his forehead on his sleeve. "Yeah." He blew out a long breath. "But I think I'm a little out of shape, too."

No way. Then Tess chided herself for noticing. "Riding takes a lot more stamina than people think."

"I'm learning that the hard way."

"We have to be very quiet, Mr. Luke," Livy warned as her voice lowered. "So not to scare the ponies."

"Okay, I'll be quiet."

They continued over the rise down to the creek and Luke couldn't help but look around at this special oasis. Vague memories flashed back to him as they passed through the large grove of aged oak trees, shading their journey. When they reached the bottom he heard the sound of water. Soon he saw the creek that ran along the edge of the trees. Tess stopped and climbed down, then helped Livy. He followed, and together they led the horses to the water, allowing them to drink.

"You can drink, too," Tess said. "The water is very good."

Luke crouched down, cupped his hands into the stream and drank the cool refreshing water. When he glanced up he caught sight of a small buckskin mare. Her mane and tail were long and shaggy, but she was a beauty.

Whiskey sounded off with a loud whinny and began to dance around nervously. Tess immediately gripped the reins to hold on to the horse.

"Whoa, boy. Slow down." Luke went to her aid as the stallion reared up. He came behind Tess and grabbed hold of the reins closer to the horse's mouth and held on tight. The powerful animal fought, desperate to answer the call of nature.

"Whoa...fella," Tess crooned, her voice low and sultry.

Luke kept his mouth shut, knowing Whiskey was her horse. Finally the cries softened as did the fight. But it was Luke's turn to feel the excitement. Tess's body was pressed against his, and their arms still entwined. Her hat had fallen off, and his face against her ear.

Damn, she smelled good.

Suddenly Whiskey's whinny brought him back to the present and the situation.

The buckskin answered back, but she wasn't alone. Off in the distance was a gray stallion. Even from far away, Luke could easily see the battle scars on the animal's hide as he pranced around nervously. Then suddenly rearing up on his hind legs, he gave a piercing whinny that echoed through the silence valley.

There was no doubt who was the alpha male in the herd. The little mare turned and ran off toward him. Whiskey gave one last neighing sound, then slowly calmed down.

"Sorry, fella," Luke said. "I think she's already taken." He glanced down at Tess. "You okay?"

She looked up at him with those deep-blue eyes. "I'm fine. Thanks for your help."

"Glad to be of service." He nodded to Whiskey. "I'd hate to see anything happen to this animal."

Taking full control of the reins, she stepped away. "That buckskin has…been around many times. But I've never seen Whiskey so…excitable before. She must be in season."

Luke couldn't help be grin. "By the attitude of the gray stallion I'd say so."

"Mommy. The pony is running away with the other ponies."

Whiskey had settled down enough, she tied him to the tree. "That's her family, sweetie."

"Oh…I thought she wanted to play with Whiskey and Dusty."

"Not today. Remember when we talked that there are times when horses mate…and make babies?"

The child nodded.

"Well, see that big gray stallion? That's the buckskin's mate. And if I let Whiskey go out there, they would have fought and one or both might have gotten hurt."

Livy seemed satisfied with the answer. She wandered down to the creek and walked along the edge.

"That was interesting."

She absently rubbed the stallion's neck. "I didn't expect to find a mare in season, or a stallion eager to fight."

Luke glanced around. He didn't remember too much about this place, but it was beautiful. A five-year-old did most of his ride around the corral. "I've heard stories about the alpha males in the herd. How sometimes they fight to the death."

"That's how it is in the wild. And I also think that's what makes this place so beautiful…so untouched…"

"And why you don't want to leave it," he finished.

"Can you look at this beautiful place and tell me that it should be destroyed. Homes constructed…roads built…and the traffic—"

He held up his hands. "Wait a minute, I never said anything about developing this land." There wasn't anyone in the business that would give him the time of day, let alone invest any money in another project with his name on it.

She turned her back to her daughter and glare at him. "You're in real estate," she said, her voice low and controlled. "Isn't that why you're so eager to sell it?"

"I *was* in real estate," he said. "Besides, I can't do a damn thing right now."

"You haven't even tried to make a go of the Rocking R. I'd say that's giving up before you give it a chance."

"But I've never ranched before in my life."

She crossed her arms over her breasts. "So, you could hire people."

"Meaning you and your father?"

Something flashed in her eyes, then it was quickly

masked. She shrugged. "It's just something to think about."

He studied her for a long time. He couldn't help but think back to another persuasive woman, one who ended up making a fool of him.

"All I'm thinking about right now is finding my brother…"

He paused when he saw two riders coming over the rise from the other side of the creek. They must be friends because Livy was waving at them.

Tess sighed. "Well, looks like it's time you met some of the neighbors."

"Who?"

"Well, Randells of course. Looks like your family has come to welcome you home."

CHAPTER THREE

HANK Barrett had lived along the Mustang Valley all of his seventy-plus years. And he'd been a neighbor of the Randell family for that same amount of time. Three of the now-grown boys, Chance, Cade and Travis, were like sons to him. Hank had been lucky enough to raise them after the loss of their mother, and their daddy had been sent to prison.

He slowed his horse as he caught sight of the couple across the creek on Rocking R property. He recognized Tess Meyers right off, and her young daughter, Livy, playing by the creek. The tall, well-built man was a stranger, although nothing made him think she was in danger as the two stood by their horses.

A closer look had Hank seeing more. The familiar way the man carried himself, the slight tilt of his hat. He smiled. So Sam's boy had returned to the valley.

Chance rode up beside Hank. "Who's that with Tess?"

Hank gave him a sideways glance. "Take a closer look."

Chance's eyes narrowed. "From a distance I'd say he looks a little like Travis. But he's in San Antonio to interview a new veterinarian."

"I'd say it's Sam's boy. Your cousin."

Chance smiled, and tiny lines fanned out around his eyes. That was about all that gave away his age of forty. The expert horseman was in top shape. He needed to be to keep up with his young family, his lovely wife, Joy, and two young daughters, Katie and Ellie, and his baby son, Jake.

"That's Luke? That skinny kid who looked like he'd cry if you said anything to him?"

Hank looked back at the couple across the creek. "I'd say that was because you and your brothers did your share of intimidating that youngster."

Chance rested his forearm on the saddle horn. "So you think he's going take over the ranch?"

Hank shrugged. "Not sure, but as head of the family, you should welcome him back."

Luke barely remembered any of his Randell cousins. Only that he was too young to hang around with them.

"Who's the old guy?"

Tess smiled. "Hank Barrett. And you better not let him hear you call him that."

Luke recognized the name. "Isn't he the one who took in my cousins?"

"And raised them. He's also your neighbor. The Circle B Ranch borders the other side, but now it's owned by Chance, Cade and Travis."

Tess smiled and waved as the two rode across the creek. "Hello, Hank. Chance."

"Tess. How are things going?"

She stood alongside a calmer Whiskey. "Can't complain."

Hank climbed down, along with the other rider, and removed his hat. Sparse patches of white hair covered his balding head. He had a friendly smile and clear hazel eyes.

"Hank, Chance, I'd like you to meet Luke Randell."

Hank was the first to respond as he offered a hand. "I knew you had to be Sam's boy." His smile disappeared. "Sorry to hear about your daddy's passing."

"Thanks." Luke shook the hand.

Next came Chance. "It's been a while, cuz."

Luke nodded. These people were strangers to him. "I've been gone a long time."

"Sorry about your father. Was he sick long?"

"I wouldn't know, I hadn't seen him in years."

"Sorry to hear that, too," Hank said, then glanced at Chance. "It's nice that you're back."

"Mr. Hank! Mr. Chance!"

They turned to see Livy come running toward them. The child couldn't get there fast enough.

"Well, if it isn't the prettiest five-year-old girl in the valley," Chance said.

Livy blushed. "What about Kate and Ellie?"

"Well, Katie is eight, and Ellie is almost six." He reached out and touched her nose. "So that leaves you."

The child turned shy and leaned into her mother. "Did you know that Whiskey almost runned off with that horse?"

"So that's the commotion we heard," Hank said, he turned to Tess. "Was it that little buckskin?"

"Yeah…that little tease," Tess said. "She finally

went back to the herd. We had a devil of a time trying to calm Whiskey."

"Yeah, he bucked and whinnied but Mommy and Mr. Luke held on tight."

Chance walked over to the bay quarter horse and rubbed his neck as he looked him over. "Man, he's a good-looking son of a gun. How is he working out?"

"He's a great horse, Chance," Tess told him. "Easy to train." She paused. "Come by the ranch and see for yourself. And I wouldn't mind some advice."

He smiled at her. "I got plenty of that, not sure if it's any good though."

For some strange reason Luke was feeling as territorial as that alpha stallion. That was crazy.

"I wouldn't even have Whiskey if it wasn't for you…and your generosity," Tess told him.

Chance pushed his hat back. "Okay, then pay me back by winning the NCHA title."

"I'm working on it. But with Dad sick, my time been limited."

"If you need any help with the herd, let us know," Chance told her. He exchanged a glance with a nodding Hank.

"The boys have taken over running things," Hank said. "These days I mostly sit around. So I've got nothing but time. I could move the herd, or help with the roundup." The old guy looked at Luke. "Son, I bet you could help some, too."

"Sure," Luke agreed. "I wouldn't mind helping out."

Chance grinned. "So city living hasn't made you soft, Luke."

For some reason the teasing rubbed Luke the wrong way. "Maybe some, but then again, I'm a lot younger than you are."

Hank burst out laughing. "You definitely are a Randell." He nudged Chance. "Come on, old man, let's get you home to your rocker." He waved, then tossed over his shoulder. "We'll stop by when you're settled in, Luke."

"Mr. Chance, will you bring Katie and Ellie to come see me?" Livy called.

"Sure, they'd like that." The men climbed on their horses and rode back up the rise.

Livy looked at her mother. "Oh boy, I get to play with Katie and Ellie."

Tess needed to calm her daughter's excitement. "Yes, honey, but Chance and Joy are pretty busy. I'm not sure how soon they'll be able to stop by."

The girl's smile disappeared. "I never have anyone to play with."

Tess knew it was lonely growing up on a ranch, but she couldn't let her daughter feel sorry for herself. "Isn't that why you got to go to the animal shelter and get Jinx?"

"I guess," the child admitted.

"And in a few weeks, you'll be starting school. You'll make all kinds of friends."

She brightened. "Will Katie and Ellie ride the bus, too?"

"I'm sure they will. And there will be other five-year-olds going to kindergarten."

Livy glanced at Luke and smiled. "And I got to go riding today. Did you have fun, Mr. Luke?"

"Yes, I did," he told her. "Thank you for letting me ride your horse."

"He's not mine, he's Grandpa's." She shook her head. "He can't ride anymore."

Tess saw the curious look on Luke's face. "I'm sorry to hear that. I hope he gets better soon."

"So do I. I miss him."

Tess didn't want to do this now…if ever. "Livy, we should get back to the house."

"Yeah, I've gotta help Aunt Bernie with the… surprise for tomorrow. You're still coming for supper, aren't you?"

"I wouldn't miss it," Luke assured her.

The child beamed. "I'm glad. And you know what else? I'm glad you came to live here, and I can see you every day."

The next day, Luke paced the kitchen, his cell phone against his ear. He'd been on the phone with Hill Air Force Base in Utah for the last twenty minutes. After getting the runaround, he'd finally reached his brother's commanding officer.

"What do you mean that you can't tell me where my brother is? Don't you know?"

"That's affirmative, sir. We know the location of Captain Randell. Since it's a…sensitive mission, he can't be reached at this time. As soon as he returns we'll give him the information."

Luke sighed. "Please, tell him it's a legal matter and urgent that he contact me. You've got my number?"

"Yes, Mr. Randell, I have it. Good day." Then the line went dead.

Luke cursed. He was tired of getting nowhere with the military. Why couldn't they just tell him his half brother was on a mission…and when he'd be back? What was strange was Brady had been notified about inheriting the ranch. Didn't he care enough to make a simple phone call?

Luke went to the window. Well, they had to settle this somehow. Was this land valuable enough for a profitable sale? Would the other Randells be interested in buying the place? Surely they'd want to keep the Rocking R in the family.

He blew out a breath. He'd never had much family to rely on. Just his mother…and she'd had so much bitterness over the divorce, it had made him gun-shy. Sam hadn't cared much about fatherhood. Luke couldn't help but wonder if it was just being *his* father?

There was a soft knocking on the screen door. He turned to find Livy standing on the porch. She had on a bright-yellow print sundress, white sneakers and ruffled socks. Her hair was up in a ponytail tied with matching ribbon.

"Mommy said I can come and get you."

"Well, hello." He held open the door, allowing the child inside. Livy didn't have a father in her life. "Mommy has no husband, and I have no Daddy," she'd told him the day he arrived.

"My, don't you look pretty as a June bug. So you're my date for the evening."

She giggled. "I can't date. Mommy said I can't until I'm older. Aunt Bernie said I'll be ready when I don't want to play with my dollies anymore and I get breasts like Mommy."

Too much information, Luke thought. "How about we just pretend for tonight?"

"'Kay. Let's go."

Luke picked up the flowers and wine off the counter. "Here, you can carry these," he said as he handed the bouquet to the wide-eyed girl.

"Oh, they're pretty."

"You can share them with Bernice and your mother."

They headed for the foreman's cottage as Livy chattered away. It was amazing how much the child could talk. What he noticed the most was how happy she seemed with her simple childhood. What about the girl's father? Did he ever visit her…or her mother? Did Tess still love the man?

Luke glanced at the simple white house the Meyers lived in. It was small, but well kept with a neatly cut lawn and colorful flowers edging the porch. Several years back another bedroom and bath had been added onto the structure. Still, it had to be crowded for four people.

"I helped Aunt Bernie plant those flowers," Livy said as they reached the front door.

"And they sure are pretty."

Livy looked up at him with those big blue eyes. "But your flowers are pretty, too."

They stepped into the living room that looked lived in, with a worn, comfortable sofa and chair. In front was a coffee table with magazines neatly stacked on the top. There was a small television in the corner.

"C'mon, Mr. Luke." She waved him on.

At the kitchen entry he was hit with mouthwatering aromas, and his stomach growled. A long table was set with simple stoneware, and steaming food was already arranged for the meal.

"Aunt Bernie, we're here." She rushed to her aunt. "Look, Mr. Luke got us flowers."

The older woman wearing an apron turned with a smile. "Well, land sakes it's been years since I've gotten flowers." She held up the multicolored bouquet. "Welcome, Luke, and thank you. They're lovely."

"Thank you for inviting me."

He suddenly felt awkward as he lifted the bottle of wine. "I also brought wine for dinner."

"Oh, my, this is a treat. I just wish I had something fancier than pot roast."

Luke grinned. "Your pot roast smells fantastic, and it's one of my favorite meals."

Bernice smiled. "Well then, let's open the wine." She went to the cabinet drawer, dug around and produced a corkscrew. "We'll celebrate your homecoming."

"Dad, please, you need to eat," Tess said as she handed him a fork.

"I'm not hungry," her father argued firmly. "Why are you always trying to get me to eat?"

Because you're losing too much weight, she screamed silently. "Because you need to keep up your strength."

"Why?" He turned those lost blue eyes on her. "I ain't goin' nowhere."

Tess blinked. Her father had been lucid most of the day. "You could go outside, or we could go for a walk." She knew that Luke had arrived, but she could skip dinner. "Want to go out to the barn? You could visit Whiskey and Dusty."

She saw a little spark in his eyes, then it quickly died. "No!" he said curtly. "What I want is to be left alone."

She tried to remember it was the illness that caused her father's erratic moods, but it still hurt her feelings.

"Okay, I'll leave you alone." Tess got up and walked to the door.

Outside in the hall, she paused, listening to the laughter coming from the kitchen. She brushed off imaginary wrinkles from her dark slacks and burgundy Western-cut blouse. With a toss of her hair off her shoulders, she put on a smile and walked in.

Her daughter was the first to see her. "Mom, look, Mr. Luke brought us flowers and wine. Aunt Bernice is drinking some, but I'm too young so I got grape juice."

"That's nice."

Luke stood. He looked so fresh in his new jeans and starched cream shirt. His inky black hair was combed back and his square jaw was clean shaven. He smiled at her and she couldn't seemed to catch her breath.

"Would you like a glass, Tess?"

She started to turn him down, then decided why not? Shouldn't she enjoy the evening, too? "That would be nice."

He filled one of her mother's crystal goblets and handed it to her. "I hope you like it."

"I'm sure I will." Those silver eyes met hers as she took a sip. Her heart leaped as the fruity liquid slid down her throat. "Very nice," she managed, and began to relax.

"Don't let it go to your head, Mommy."

They all burst into laughter.

"Well, Aunt Bernie said that she didn't want it to go to her head."

Tess looked at Luke and felt her body warm. The wine wasn't her problem…. "I'll try not to, honey," she told her daughter.

"Since we're all here, why don't we sit down to supper," her aunt suggested.

Luke helped Livy to her seat. "I'm sorry to hear that Mr. Meyers isn't well enough to join us."

Tess glanced at Bernice. "No, he's not feeling well this evening."

"Grandpa has been sick a long time."

Bernice set the rolls on the table. "Livy, will you say the blessing tonight?"

She held out her hand. "Mr. Luke, you got to hold my hand and Mommy's hand. So God will know we're all praying."

"Okay," he said.

Tess felt a strange tingle go up her arm as Luke grasped her hand. She blamed it on the wine.

"Close your eyes," Livy coaxed. "Lord, please bless our food you gave us, and thank you for taking care of Grandpa and bringing Mr. Luke here. Amen."

Everyone else said, "Amen." Then the food started around the table. Tess watched as Luke helped serve Livy. The girl thrived on the male attention. Maybe more so since her grandfather hadn't been around.

Tess took another sip of wine. The last thing she wanted was her daughter getting attached to a man who wasn't going to stay around. Tess couldn't, either. She'd survived one man leaving…never again.

More laughter broke out, and she shook away her thoughts. She took the bowl of potatoes and dished up a large helping along with meat and gravy.

"Bernice, this is the best pot roast I've ever eaten," Luke told her.

Her aunt blushed. "Oh, I bet you tell all the ladies that."

Luke arched an eyebrow. "Not about their pot roast, I don't." He got up and retrieved the bottle off the counter and added to their glasses.

Bernice laughed. "You're a sweet-talkin' rascal, Luke Randell."

Tess couldn't believe her aunt's behavior. She was actually flirting with the man. She glanced at Livy. In her little-girl way, her daughter was doing the same.

Luke lifted his glass. "I'd like to make a toast. To three of the loveliest ladies I've ever had the pleasure of dining with."

Livy climbed onto her knees and clinked her glass with Luke, Bernice and then to her. "Mommy, you do it, too."

Tess turned to the handsome man to find him watching her as she touched her glass with the other three. Accidentally her fingers brushed Luke's and she felt the strangest sensation. Warmth went through her and suddenly her stomach did a flip. It's the wine, she told herself as she quickly went back to her meal. She had no business having any feelings whatsoever for this man.

A few minutes later Livy spoke up. "Aunt Bernie is it time yet?" she asked. "I ate all my food."

"Okay, it's time." The two got up from the table and went to the covered cake pedestal on the counter. Bernice removed the lid to reveal a chocolate masterpiece. With Livy's assistance, her aunt carried it to the table.

"Look, Mr. Luke, it's chocolate, your favorite. Aunt Bernie and me baked it for you."

"It sure is. And the prettiest cake I've ever seen. And I can't wait to taste it."

Livy beamed, and Tess couldn't help but feel sad that she'd denied her daughter a father. Even if it wasn't her fault that the man she'd thought she loved didn't love her or his child.

Tess quickly shook away the memories. This evening was too nice to think about anything bad. "I can't wait to taste it, too."

"Mommy, did you know that chocolate was Mr. Luke's very favorite?"

"No, I didn't," Tess said. "Aren't you a lucky girl, because isn't chocolate your favorite, too."

The child nodded at Luke. She was obviously enamored by the good-looking Randell. So was her mother, but at least Tess knew enough to keep her distance.

Bernice cut everyone a piece and handed them out. She picked up another plate.

Luke took a bite. "This is wonderful."

Livy put a forkful in her mouth. "Mmmmmm. It's good."

Luke grinned at her, then turned and winked at Tess. "You should try some," he urged.

She managed to take a bite. The rich flavor melted in her mouth. She had to fight back a groan. It was a sad state of affairs when a grown woman who was nearly thirty got her pleasure from eating a piece of cake.

She stole a glance at Luke. She bet he knew how to give a woman pleasure. She gasped, realizing the dangerous direction of her thoughts.

Thirty minutes later, dressed in pajamas, Livy was snuggled in her single bed covered with a Little Kitty comforter. The matching lamp sent off a soft glow, just enough to read some of her daughter's favorite story.

Already the child's eyes were drooping. "I'm too tired for a story, Mommy." She fought a yawn. "I like Mr. Luke."

"I'm glad," Tess said, knowing she hated to see her daughter get attached to a near stranger.

"I'm glad he came to live here."

Tess wouldn't go that far. Luke Randell's arrival would change their life, but she couldn't explain that to a five-year-old. "You've had a busy day. It's time for sleep."

"I can't yet. I forgot to say good-night to Mr. Luke."

Tess recognized her daughter's familiar pout. "Mr. Luke has probably already gone home, sweetie."

Livy blinded at tears. "No, he didn't, he's helping Aunt Bernie do the dishes. Please…"

Tess knew she shouldn't let her daughter get away with having her way, but it was late. "Okay, I'll see if he's here." She got up and went out to the kitchen. That was where she found Luke and Bernice standing by the sink, laughing.

She realized she was a little jealous of their relaxed and easy banter. It was something she was never good at…especially with men.

Tess started to back away when Luke looked at her. His smile faded. "Is Livy asleep already?"

"She's in bed, but if you don't mind, she wants to say good-night."

He smiled. "Of course not." He set the towel on the counter. "I'll be right back, Bernice. So don't try to put away that heavy platter."

He walked toward her and Tess felt a warming sensation rush through her. Please…let it be the wine. She turned and he followed her down the narrow hall.

Luke stopped at the partly open door. He gave a quick glance at Tess. He could see how protective she was of her young daughter. He didn't blame her.

"She's nearly asleep."

"I won't stay long," he assured her and walked into the room. He went straight to the small bed. At first he thought the child was asleep, but her eyes opened.

"Oh, Mr. Luke, you came."

He eased down to the side of the bed. "I couldn't leave without saying good-night to you, shortcake."

She smiled. "I like it that you call me that name."

"Okay, then I'll keep calling you that. Shortcake." He took her hand. "Now, I think I better leave before your mother chases me out. Good-night, Livy. Thanks for inviting me." He couldn't say why he leaned down and placed a kiss on her cheek.

"'Night, Mr. Luke." What he didn't expect was that the little girl would kiss him back and wrap those tiny arms around his neck. His chest tightened with emotion. How had she managed to sneak in and steal a piece of his heart in just a few short days?

He stood and left the room to find Tess waiting for him. "She's a special little girl."

"I know," Tess said. "I'm protective of her, too."

Luke didn't blame her for that. "Is that because of her father?"

Tess straightened. "He's never been a part of her life. That's fine with me. It's just been me and her… and my dad."

"My mother raised me alone, too. I believe everyone knows of my father's affair." Hell, why was he bringing this up now?

"There are a lot of single mothers out there," Tess said.

Luke knew he was crazy for letting himself be drawn to this woman. Yet, nothing he did seemed to stop it. He took a step closer to her. "The guy must have been out of his mind to let you go."

He heard her quick intake of breath as her blue eyes widened in surprise. But before she could speak, Bernice appeared from the other end of the hall.

"Ray's not in his room," she announced.

Tess moved away from Luke, trying to remain calm. "It's okay. He probably just went outside."

Bernice nodded. "His window was open. He must have climbed out."

Luke came up behind her. "Is there a problem with him going out?"

Tess sighed, trying desperately to clear her head. "Dad can't be left alone. He has the early stages of Alzheimer's disease."

CHAPTER FOUR

TESS'S heart pounded in her chest as she took off out the door and ran around the house and yard. With no sign of her dad, she widened the search area. She heard her name called out, but refused to stop.

Dad was out there…alone, and she had to find him. Only the porch light and gathering clouds overhead helped illuminate the familiar path to the barn. The wind had picked up and it smelled like rain.

Not good. She was trembling when she reached the barn. She struggled with the heavy door when suddenly Luke's steady hands took over the job.

"Tess…we'll find him," Luke assured her. For some strange reason his words reassured her. "I'm going to help you."

"It's okay, he's probably in the barn with Dusty," she lied. Anyway, her dad was her responsibility.

"Has he wandered off before?"

She shook her head, and started the trek down the aisle. An overhead light guided the way. She hated to share her private life with a virtual stranger.

"He had hip surgery about a year ago and was laid

up. That's when we discovered the other problem." The horses stirred, and she knew something had disturbed them.

"Dad!" Tess called as she reached Dusty's empty stall and another wave of fear hit her. She swung around and hurried out into the corral. A security light came on, but the area was deserted, too, and the gate was open.

Tess cupped her hands around her mouth. "Dad!" she yelled into the windy blackness. She ran into the field, trying to control her panic, but how could she when her dad was out there all alone. He could fall in a ravine or…

Luke caught up and grabbed her arm. "Tess, wait."

She tried to break his strong hold. "I've got to find him."

"You can't, it's black as pitch out there."

"And my dad is out there somewhere."

Luke gripped her other arm and shook her slightly. He had to calm her down. "I know he is. But you can't go running off."

"I know the land."

"And when you find him you'll probably need help to bring him back. Besides, he's on horseback." It was too dark to see her fear, but he felt her tremble. "Do you have any idea where he could have ridden off to? A favorite place?" He was frustrated he couldn't do more. "Is it possible your dad saddled a horse?"

She shook her head. "Dad's riding Dusty bareback. The bridle was missing from outside his stall. That's all he needs since those two have been partnered for twenty years."

"That's good. Maybe Dusty will bring him back," he said, trying to encourage her.

"I'm more concerned about Dad falling off the horse. He isn't real strong these days."

"Okay, then we should call for help."

"Please, don't call the sheriff, yet. I'm going to look for him."

He nodded at her stubbornness. "Okay. I'm going with you."

"No. You don't know your way around the ranch."

He followed her back to the barn. "Take it or leave it, Tess, because I'm not letting you go by yourself. If Ray did fall off Dusty and is hurt, you can't manage him by yourself."

Tess blinked at threatening tears. This was all her fault. She should have watched him closer. "Okay, but you better keep up."

"I will. He followed her into the tack room. She assigned him a saddle for Lady. Luke took it from the stand and went to the mare's stall. When they finished, Bernice and Livy came in with rain ponchos and flashlights, plus a pair of jeans and riding boots for Tess. Hats for both of them.

Bernice looked worried. "I saw you in the corral alone so I called Hank Barrett to help. It was lucky that Chance, Cade and Travis were there for supper."

Tess sighed in frustration. She didn't usually ask for help, but this was her father. "Where are they going to meet us?"

"Hank said they'd start from the Mustang Valley and spread out until they reached you." She also handed her niece the cell phone. "I programmed in Chance's number, and he has yours. They'll call if—when they see anything." Aunt Bernice hugged her. "It's going to be all right. And you've got Luke to help you."

"Thanks, Bernice." She went back to the tack room to change.

Livy tugged on Luke's hand. "Mr. Luke. Will you bring my grandpa back?"

Luke crouched down to be eye level with Livy. He definitely wasn't the hero type. Yet, seeing the child's pleading look, he knew he'd give it everything he had. "I'll do my best."

"Here's some licorice." She pulled out a small bag. "It's Grandpa's favorite."

"I'm sure he'll be happy to get this." He stuffed the sack into his shirt pocket and stood, then grabbed Lady's reins and headed outside.

Tess came out of the tack room, said her goodbyes, then together they walked the horses out and mounted them.

"Your mare will stay close to me," Tess told him and glanced up at the sky. "Let's hope the rain holds off for a while." She gave Luke her cell number in case they got separated.

They exchanged a long look. Luke's chest tightened, feeling protective toward her…more than he had a right to. Finally she glanced away and they went through the gate.

"We're going to find him, Tess," he recited the mantra. "We'll find him."

She nodded as they rode through the trees. "Dad's going to hate us coming to look for him. He's very proud."

Luke heard the tears in her voice, he also heard the love in her words. "He sounds like quite a man. I can't wait to meet him."

Luke prayed he'd get the chance.

About twenty minutes later they met up with Hank about a mile from the creek. A light drizzle had begun and they'd put on their rain ponchos.

"Hi, Hank."

"Tess. Luke." He sighed. "I hate to say it, but we haven't seen any sign of Ray." He raised his hand. "The boys are still sweeping the ridge on both sides."

"We came straight here," Tess told him. "I've whistled for Dusty several times, but nothing." She wiped the back of her wrist over her wet face. "I can't believe Dad could have gone this far. He was only left alone while we were eating supper."

"You can't watch him every minute, Tess," Hank said, leaving any other comments about Ray Meyers' rapidly progressing illness unsaid.

Suddenly a rider came over the rise leading a horse. "It's Dusty," she said hopefully.

It was Travis Randell who arrived with the riderless gelding. "I found Ray's horse, but there's no sign of your dad. Sorry. Cade is still looking, and Chance is out there, too."

He looked at Luke. "I take it you're Luke?" He held out his hand. "Hi, I'm Travis."

Luke shook his hand. "Nice to meet you. Wish it was under better circumstances."

Travis nodded. "We'll stay out here as long as it takes."

"Where did you find Dusty?" Tess asked.

"That strip of north pasture bordering Chance's ranch. It's about a mile from here."

Luke turned to Tess. "We should ride out there," he suggested.

"Yeah, I want to go." She took Dusty's reins, but before she could leave, Hank reached over to stop her departure.

"The weather is only going to get worse, Tess," he told her. "I think we better call in the sheriff."

Tess tried not to think about the danger, but she had to. "Okay, but I'm going to check the old shack up in the foothills. If he isn't there, I'll call the sheriff myself."

"Are you talking about Jake Randell's old shack? I didn't know the place was still standing." Hank looked at Travis. "Did you or your brothers come across a shack?"

"No, we didn't see anything."

Luke sat back in his saddle feeling useless. Suddenly he remembered a small cabin along a little creek. It was his grandfather's place. "I think my dad took me there once."

"I know exactly where it is," Tess said as Whiskey danced anxiously. "We'll call you when we get there."

Hank nodded. "We just want this to be a happy ending. Let us know if you need more help."

Luke looked at Travis. "Thank you both, and thank your brothers for us."

"Not a problem." The young Randell smiled. "It's a pretty tight community here. Ray and Tess would do the same for us. Good luck."

Tess rode off leading Dusty trailing behind. Luke right behind her. The rain had grown heavier, but it didn't slow their pace. Luke was glad he'd been able to keep up. He glanced at Tess. He knew she was stressed, but she hadn't lost her composure. She was the most self-sufficient woman he'd ever met. Not to mention stubborn, headstrong…graceful…beautiful. Why would she lead him to believe that Ray only had a temporary illness?

Was she hoping to renew the ranch lease, and she thought he'd discriminate against her because she was woman? Man or woman, he wasn't planning to renew the Meyerses' lease.

With that decision, he'd be throwing out two women, a small child and a sick father. Why not? Hadn't he done it with investment properties in Dallas? He'd gotten into the real estate business to make money, not to be charitable.

He tried to tell himself that he needed to make a living. When had he gotten so greedy? Now there was nothing but this ranch.

It was funny that the last place he'd ever wanted to return to was the only home he had left. He looked at the woman ahead of him. Technically it was Tess's home more than his. And right now she had a lot more to lose.

Tess slowed her horse as they approached a group of trees. Luke wiped his eyes and saw a small structure. He took out the flashlight to guide them the rest of the way. They reached the shack and climbed down, then tied the horses to the old hitching post under a sagging lean-to. It was good enough to keep them out of the weather.

Luke took the one step on the landing and pushed

open the stubborn door. He shone the flashlight inside to find an old table and chairs placed by a potbelly stove. He moved the light along the wall and that was where he saw the huddled form on the bunk. An old man held up his hand against the glare from the light. "Shut that damn thing off."

"Dad!" Tess cried running to him, stripping off her poncho as she reached the bunk.

Luke set the flashlight on the table, giving Tess more illumination to check her father's condition.

Ray Meyers was a slight man with thinning, white hair plastered to his head. His face was lined, no doubt by hard work…and life.

"Dad, are you all right?"

The shivering man refused to look at her. "I can't find my way back."

"Dad, it's me, Tess." Her gaze scanned over him, making sure he wasn't hurt. "You're safe now, and I'm going to take you home."

"Home?" His eyes searched her face, then suddenly he blinked and gripped her hand. "I can't go back there. Elizabeth is gone."

Luke looked at Tess to see her tears as she stroked her father's hand. "Oh, Dad, Mom's been gone for a long time."

The old man's eyes widened in recognition. "Tess… Oh, Tess… She got sick." Suddenly he shook his head and began to sob. "I couldn't help her. I miss her."

"I know, Dad. I miss her, too." Tess climbed up on the bed and wrapped her arms around him.

Emotion clogged Luke's throat. He moved back,

then stepped outside to give them some privacy. He busied himself checking the animals, then he untied the bed rolls and brought them into the cabin. Inside he checked to be sure the blankets were dry and handed one to Tess.

Taking the extra flashlight, he went back outside and found pieces of wood stacked under the lean-to. Sorting through the bundle, he found some wood chips dry enough to burn.

On his return trip, he found Tess cradling her sleeping father. "There are matches in my saddle bag," she said softly. "I need to call Hank and Bernice."

"I can do that for you," he said as he took her cell phone. He went back outside and made the call. He thanked Hank again and assured him they could get Ray back to the house without help. Could they? Would the man be lucid enough for the ride back? He then talked with Bernice and let her know the situation.

Carrying an armful of wood inside, he placed it in the ancient stove, then added some wadded-up newspaper from the floor. There was no doubt that someone had been using the cabin recently. He lit a match and tossed it into the stove, and the paper caught fire instantly. After it got going, he closed the grated cast iron door and pulled off his plastic poncho. The rain had caused the temperature to drop ten to fifteen degrees.

Luke also lit the kerosene lantern on the table and glanced across the room to find Tess watching him. Seeing her sadness caused his chest to tighten. He wanted to go to her, take her in his arms. "This should help take the chill off," he told her. The fire from the stove and lantern had helped illuminate the tiny cabin.

He doubted the warmth he felt was from the wood burning. Suddenly the rain grew heavy, pounding rhythmically against the tin roof, breaking the spell between them.

He glanced overhead. "Looks like we're not going anywhere for a while."

"Then it's good Dad's asleep." She lifted Ray's head and slid away from him, gently laying him down on the dirty mattress. The old man curled up in a fetal position and began to snore softly.

Tess looked at Luke, but avoided his eyes. "I know it's not exactly sanitary, but…he needs to rest. And he's warm." She went to the door and squeezed through the small opening to the outside.

Luke was at a loss for what else to do for her. He went to the door and hesitated…until he heard her quiet sobs. He stepped out under the overhang.

"Tess…" He spoke her name and touched her shoulder.

She turned around, her head lowered, trying to hide her weakness. "It's okay, let it go."

She shook her head and frantically swiped at her tears. "I can't. He…needs me. My family…needs me."

Luke had no idea what that was like. He'd never had much family. He'd never gotten so involved with anyone so they would have to depend on him. This was different…Tess was different. He wanted to be there for her.

He knew she was too proud to ask for help. "What about you, Tess? What do you need?"

She finally raised her head. In the shadowed darkness,

he could see her tear-stained cheeks, her sadness. Her eyes revealed so much: her need…her desire. It also made him realize how long he'd been alone.

"I can't need anything," she breathed.

"Then let me offer it," he told her. "Let me help you, Tess."

He took a step closer and drew her against him. He closed his eyes when her luscious body pressed into his. She resisted at first, but then her arms slipped around his waist and she buried her face in his shirt. Then she let go and cried her heart out.

He blinked his own tears away in the dark and rain. She was losing her father…piece by piece. The man who'd raised her by himself. Maybe Luke was feeling his own pain, too, about the loss of his own parent.

Her crying slowed, then stopped as she looked up at him. The darkness hid her vulnerability, but not the intimacy created between them.

"I'm sorry," she whispered. "I guess I lost it."

He cupped her cheek. "It's okay, Tess. I've got you." Unable to stop what was happening, he lowered his head…and his mouth caressed her lips. Her soft gasp drew him back for more. His mouth touched hers again…and again, until she joined in. She raised up and wrapped her arms around his neck, parting her lips so he could delve inside to taste her sweetness.

He groaned and widened his stance, pulling her closer. She made him hungry…so hungry. He sipped from her, unable to think about anything else but her taste, her touch…her body pressed against his. It would be so easy to lose himself in her.

Finally she broke off the kiss and they were both breathing hard.

Tess finally stepped back. "I've got to check on Dad." She rushed inside.

Luke took another calming breath and released it, hoping the cool air would help him. It didn't. He suddenly realized that not much could help him when it came to Tess Meyers.

Two hours later the rain had lessened some, but there was no way to bring a vehicle into the area. So they were stuck here until the rain stopped. Probably dawn.

Tess sat on the opposite end of the bed covered with the other blanket. Dad was still sleeping soundly. There was no chance for her, not after her foolishness. How could she let Luke kiss her? She couldn't blame him alone; she'd participated in that kiss, too. What she needed to concentrate on was her future, not start something with the new ranch owner.

She stole a glance across the room at Luke who was seated on the floor by the stove. His head was tilted back against the roughly paneled wall. His eyes were closed, but she doubted he was sleeping, either.

"You should try and get some sleep," Luke said, his voice sound so intimate in the small quarters.

"I can't...I worried about Dad."

"I think it's more than that." There was a long pause. "It's okay, Tess," Luke began. "We're consenting adults and unattached. There's no sin in sharing a kiss."

"It still shouldn't have happened." She paused. "I don't want you to think that it will lead anywhere."

He hesitated, then said, "You mean like you sneaking off in the dead of night to my house…and me having my way with you?"

She heard the amusement in his voice. "In your dreams, Randell."

Luke wasn't smiling. She'd been in his thoughts and daydreams since he'd first found her in his bedroom. Tess had ignited something in him he didn't want to analyze. And the kiss they'd shared told him he should definitely back away…far away. "Don't worry, Tess, it was only a kiss," he lied, knowing he'd intended to offer comfort but it had turned out to be much more.

"Just so you know, all I want is a business relationship."

He snorted as he thought back to his past experiences. He might be cynical, but people take advantage if they have the chance. "Good. That should get us through the next few months."

Tess needed to concentrate on her dad, not on the man across the room who'd awakened feelings in her, feelings she thought had died when Ben had walked away from her and his child. Worse, she'd let Luke distract her from her responsibilities. She couldn't let that happen again.

Her dad stirred on the bunk and sat up.

"Dad, are you okay?" She reached for him, but he pushed her hand away.

"I'm just dandy." He threw the blanket off and scooted off the bunk. "I just need to go outside a minute."

Tess followed him. "I'll help you."

"No, I'm not an invalid yet, girl. And I don't need any help to answer the call of nature."

Before Tess could answer, Luke climbed to his feet. "You know, I need to take that trip, too. You mind if I go with you?"

Ray looked up. "Who the hell are you?"

"Luke Randell. I arrived at the ranch a few days ago."

Her father studied him. "You Sam's boy?"

A smile appeared. "Yes, I am. It's nice to meet you, sir." Luke held out his hand to shake her father's hand and helped him to his feet. She was grateful for Luke's kindness. Her father hated being babied by the women of the family.

"You resemble your daddy. There's plenty of Randells around these parts."

Luke nodded. "I think the rain has let up so we shouldn't get too wet."

Her father looked old and stooped next to the tall well-built younger man. He also had a slight limp from his hip surgery last year as they made their way to the door.

After they answered the call of nature, Luke helped Ray back onto the porch. He hadn't had any experience with Alzheimer's patients, but as far as he could tell, for the moment anyway, Ray Meyers's mind was clear.

The older man hesitated at the door and glanced toward the horses. "Mr. Randell, could you do me a favor?"

"Only if you call me Luke."

Ray nodded. "Could you tell me how I got out here?"

"It seems you wanted to go for a ride on Dusty." Luke turned to the older man. "Do you remember anything?"

He looked frustrated. "Just bits and pieces. Did I hurt Dusty?" At the sound of his friend speaking his name, the horse bobbed his head and neighed.

Luke smiled. "Dusty's fine. We were worried you might have taken a fall, though."

"I feel all right…but I sure as hell don't remember getting here." He wiped his hand over his face. "Oh, man, I probably scared my girl half to death."

"The main thing is that you're safe. That's all she cares about."

"I'm worthless like this. I can't even stay on a horse."

"I know Tess doesn't think of you like that. I'd say you're a lucky man to have three females who love you so much."

"I should be taking care of them, not the other way around. Maybe she should just put me in a nursing home."

"That's something you need to talk over with your family. Right now, I think we better get you back home."

Just then Tess came out of the cabin. "Luke's right. I want us to get home. You can ride Whiskey, since he has a saddle. I'll take Dusty."

Luke watched Ray start to argue, but then he nodded. "I wouldn't mind sleeping in my own bed."

They put out the fire and closed up the line shack and finally were on their way. The rain had stopped and the clouds moved out, giving them a moonlit sky and a clearer path back to the ranch. They still moved slowly.

Once they pulled up in front of the small house, Luke helped Ray off his horse, tied them to the post, then walked up to the porch. Bernice met them at the door.

"Well, it's about time you got home," she said. "You worried us all to death."

Ray frowned. "See what I have to put up with?"

"I'd say you've got it pretty good."

They continued down the hall and into the bedroom. Luke started to leave when little Livy stepped out of her room. She was wearing a nightgown and holding a raggedy stuffed animal.

"Hi, shortcake." He bent down. "Shouldn't you be asleep?"

She nodded. "I want to thank you for bringing Grandpa home." She threw her arms around his neck and hugged him tight, then she placed a kiss on his cheek. "'Night, Mr. Luke." She turned and disappeared into her room.

Before Luke could recover Bernice appeared. "Thank you, Luke." She hugged and kissed him, too, then went back into Ray's bedroom.

He didn't quite know how to handle this. Then Tess appeared. Those blue eyes bore into his and he began to ache. He knew the feelings she could create in him…if he let her. "I guess you're next," he teased lightly, but wanted that kiss and hug more than he could admit.

She strolled past him. "You'll get a thank you from me," she said. "Anything else— Like I said earlier in your dreams, Randell, in your dreams."

CHAPTER FIVE

SMILING, Luke followed Tess out of the house. As she started to lead the horses to the barn, he took Lady's reins from her.

"What are you doing?" she asked.

"It's called helping out."

"You don't have to, I can do it."

"I know. You're superwoman." Leading the horses, they walked side by side toward the barn. "It's okay, Tess, if someone helps you."

"It's the middle of the night, and you could be in bed."

He didn't need her using that terminology. "So I get there a little later. I can always sleep in." He had nowhere to go…no job. "You, on the other hand, will have to be up in a few hours to feed the stock."

Tess didn't respond as he slid open the barn door and they escorted the horses to their stalls. She removed Whiskey's saddle and wiped him down, then went to Dusty. She glanced over to see Luke following her actions with Lady. Once finished, they carried the saddles into the tack room.

Tess didn't know how to handle this. Luke Randell

was nothing like she'd had expected. She'd figured he would arrive here, live in the big ranch house and keep to himself while he decided what to do with the place. She never expected the man to get involved with her… problems…her life.

With the tack put away and the horses settled, they headed out of the barn to the house. It was where Tess would feel safe. After tonight, she felt so exposed to this man. In just the few days that Luke had been at the Rocking R, he'd learned far too much about her—about her dreams…and now her family secrets. He hadn't flinched, even when he learned about her father's illness.

Then he had to go and kiss her. Big mistake on her part. What she needed was to keep her concentration on her family and her horse breeding business. Not on another man who would eventually walk out of her life.

"You know, there are programs out there that might help your dad," Luke said.

"Dad has been resistant about doing anything but sitting in his room. Until tonight."

"Maybe if he spent more time outside doing things."

She stopped at the porch. "Look, Luke, I'll do about anything to help my father, but I also have to work with the horses. If he's outside there's a lot that can happen to him. He could get hurt." She hated people coming around and telling her how to handle the illness. "As you can see, I did a lousy job tonight."

When she turned away, he reached for her. "I wasn't judging you, Tess. I can't imagine how you do all you do on your own as it is. I just want you to know there's help out there.

She tensed. "I'm not putting him in a nursing home."

He raised a calming hand. "I'm not suggesting that. But there are other options. There are exercise programs and medications that might help him."

She sighed and closed her eyes. She was tired. "I plan to talk to his doctor tomorrow when I take him in."

Luke smiled and she felt a warm tingle rush through her. "Good. Now if you leave instructions on feeding the horses, I can handle that for you."

It would be so easy to lean on him. "That's okay, I can do it."

"I know you can, but that doesn't mean I can't help. 'Night, Tess."

Tess watched him walk off the porch and head toward the big house. She didn't go inside until the shadowy figure disappeared, fighting the urge to call him back. She wasn't used to depending on anyone but herself and her family. And never a man she could fall hard for… that was far too dangerous.

At dawn Luke left his house and headed for the barn. Once inside he checked on the horses. All three were valuable animals and seemed to have fasred well during the rain-soaked night.

"You're glad to be back in your dry stall, huh, fella?" He patted Whiskey and was happy the stallion seemed comfortable around him. They also expected him to fill their feed buckets.

"Sorry, you have to wait for the boss lady."

At that moment the door opened and Tess strolled in. Dressed in jeans and a navy-blue Henley shirt, she looked fresh from the shower with her blond hair pulled back into a ponytail. She had just enough of a sleepy-eyed look to stir his body and make him wish for another activity this morning.

If she was surprised to see him there, she didn't show it. "If you're going to help, then you better come with me."

Luke followed her as she went to the plastic bins where she kept the grain. She instructed him on the amount of feed for each of the horses. Then she showed him a wheelbarrow and a pitchfork and sent him off to start mucking out a stall. He caught her surprise as he went off to do the job. About an hour later they'd finished all the chores and were headed back to the house.

Luke started toward his house when Tess called to him. "Bernice would shoot me if I didn't ask you in for breakfast."

He grinned, feeling his strained muscles and his hunger. "We can't have that, can we?" He hurried to catch up with her, and they headed through the back door.

Bernice beamed at him. "Good morning, Luke."

"It is a good morning, Bernice." He pulled off his hat and hung it on the hook as did Tess. He went to the sink and washed his hands. "I hope you don't mind me coming by."

"The way you helped out last night, I wouldn't mind you coming by every day."

Luke dried his hands on a towel and took a seat at the table. "I wouldn't want to wear out my welcome." He smiled, glancing at a stoic Tess. "But you might be able to persuade me with some of your cooking."

"You charming devil." She placed a stack of pancakes in front of him. "I'm surprised some woman hasn't snapped you up."

"Maybe I haven't found the right woman." He took a bite and groaned. "Oh, my, I think I have. Bernice, you have to marry me."

Laughing, Bernice waved a dismissive hand. "Oh, yeah, you're definitely a charmer, just like all those other Randell boys."

An hour later, with his stomach full, Luke walked back to his house. Funny, for a man who'd pretty much been a loner most of his life, he found he didn't want to leave the Meyerses' kitchen. Even Livy and her grandfather had joined in the meal.

He walked through the back door and was hit with silence. He'd noticed it before, but more so now after spending time with a family. This house was big…and empty.

All these years his mother had insisted that no one live in her house. He understood some of Kathleen Randell's resentment over her husband's affair, but why would she want to hang on to a place that reminded her of so much unhappiness?

It also made him realize how empty his life was. He'd lost everything, and there weren't many people who cared. His thoughts turned to Gina. She was supposed to have loved him. Yet she bailed out…when her father pulled out of the deal. She took off six months ago, and he realized he didn't even miss her. It made him wonder if he'd ever loved her.

He walked down the hall through the formal dining

room with the dark wainscoting and paneling and oversize furniture. At the stairs, he went up to the second floor and the master bedroom where he'd been sleeping since he returned home. There was a four-poster bed and dresser, but there weren't any personal things left in the room that had once been his parents. He hadn't checked the drawers, knowing his mother's will stated that all the contents of this house were his. Since her death, three years ago, Luke had never wanted to come back here. Now he hadn't had any choice.

He tugged his shirt out of his jeans, knowing after the workout in the barn, a shower would be a good idea. He pulled out clean clothes from his suitcase in the corner and headed for the bathroom.

Ten minutes later he returned to the bedroom. He had other things to do, but nothing would take his mind off Tess and her dad. He wanted to go with her, but he knew she wouldn't ask for help. He told himself that he was just trying to help out a nice family. That wasn't entirely true. There were so many reasons why he should keep away from her.

Their relationship was supposed to be business only. He needed to remember the woman who had helped destroy him. Good old Gina.

"You need to focus on rebuilding your career… your credibility," he reminded himself. Besides, he was nearly broke. He owned half a ranch, but couldn't locate the brother he'd never met. Not exactly a perfect life.

He walked to the bank of windows that overlooked the barn and corral. The worst part was he was beginning to like it here. And he couldn't let that happen. He didn't do home and family very well.

His attention was drawn to a late-model truck coming through the gate. It stopped by the barn, and a tall man climbed out. He smiled to himself. Looked like one of the Randells had come for a visit.

He headed downstairs, grabbed a hat off the hook and met Chance on the back porch, surprised to find the big cowboy was holding the hand of a little girl. Pretty and petite, she was dressed in blue jean shorts and a white shirt with ruffles. Her long blond hair was pulled back with clips.

"Hey, how are you doing this morning?" his cousin asked.

"I'm fine."

Chance nodded. "Luke, this is my six-year-old daughter, Ellie. Ellie, this is our cousin Luke."

The cute child smiled at him, but stayed close to her father. "Hi." She looked up at her dad. "Can I go play with Livy now?"

"She's a little shy with strangers," his cousin told him as they both watched until the child reached the cottage and went inside.

"Tess isn't here," Luke announced. "She took Ray to the doctor this morning."

"I know. I talked to her earlier."

Luke frowned. Had Tess called him for help?

Chance sighed and pushed his hat back, revealing his brown hair. "It's a rough situation all around. I wanted Tess to know that we'll help her out whenever she needs us."

Luke figured Chance meant the entire Randell family. "I'll pass on the word to her."

Chance smiled. "I'll be here to tell her myself, since I'm going to work Whiskey this morning."

Luke couldn't even speak as Chance took off toward the barn, then stopped at looked back at him. "If you want, you're welcome to come along." His cousin gave him the once-over. "Last night you handled yourself pretty good on a horse."

Luke's competitiveness had him hurrying after his cousin. "I hadn't ridden since I left here."

"Some things are bred in you. Like I said, you did real well." They paused at the door as Chance said, "You know, all the wives are asking about you."

"Really. What are they asking?"

Chance shook his head. "I'll let them ask you the questions," he said. "I'm just to pass on an invitation to a barbecue to you and of course, the Meyers family, too."

"When?"

"Tonight." Chance grinned. "You might as well get it over with. The women in this family can be relentless when they want something."

"What about Ray?" Luke walked through the barn door. "I'm not sure he could handle the big crowd."

"Then we'll bring the get-together here."

Luke blinked.

"Don't worry. We'll bring everything we need, including a barbecue grill. So come on, you can ride Dusty. He's a pro at cutting."

Luke was swept along but had a feeling Chance had

it planned that way. He'd give his cousin this one, but he'd get even. After all he was a Randell, too.

Tess returned from the doctor just before noon. She sat while her dad had lunch, and listened to Livy and Ellie talk about their adventures that morning.

Thirty minutes later she was on her way to the barn to see what else had gone on while she was away. No one was inside…and Dusty and Whiskey were missing from their stalls. She went out to the corral, and that was where she found them.

Standing in the shadows, no one noticed her as she watched Luke. The one-time city guy surprised her as he worked Dusty. He sat relaxed in the saddle while the horse went through the maneuvers of cutting a calf from the dozen in the herd.

Chance was a horse breeder and trainer by profession, and he was excellent at both. He called out instructions and encouragement to his cousin, and Luke did exactly what was asked of him. Surprisingly, he had an easy command of the horse and they worked well as a team. Luke sat relaxed in the saddle, his hands on the horn and the reins slack. He was letting the horse do what he was trained for.

"Use your legs to give the commands," Chance instructed.

The deep concentration showed on Luke's face as he never took his eyes off the anxious calf. Finally the yearling relented and the task was complete.

"Good job, cuz," Chance called out as he rode up to him. "What do you think, Tess? He got the makings of a cowboy?"

Caught, she had no choice but to come out of hiding. Tess straightened, stepped out into the sunlight and walked toward the men on horseback. The calf scurried back to the herd across the pen. "He might have some potential," she called out over the bawling of the cows.

Luke looked pleased at her back-handed compliment.

"Not bad for a city boy," Chance teased.

She rubbed Whiskey's neck. "What do you think of this guy? Did you get a chance to work him?"

"I sure did. He's something, all right. I think it's time you put him to a real test. Enter him in a show."

Tess's heart raced with excitement. Those were the words she'd wanted to hear. "He's ready, huh?"

Chance nodded. "I wouldn't say it if I didn't think he was ready. At least see how Whiskey does in competition. He's got to learn how to handle the crowds. Start locally at the San Angelo Rodeo and work your way up."

Luke saw her hesitation. "Isn't this what you wanted?"

Tess straightened. "It is, but I have other concerns right now. Dad needs me."

Both Chance and Luke climbed off their mounts. It was Chance who spoke first. "What did the doctor say, if you don't mind my asking?"

She glanced at Luke, then back at his cousin. "No, I don't mind." She released a breath. "After I told him about Dad wandering off last night, he was concerned, especially about Dad's depression. The doctor wants him to come back Monday for a series of tests. Right now he said Dad needs to get out of his room and get more exercise."

Chance didn't hesitate. "Okay, that sounds good. What can we do to help?"

Tess shook her head. "You've already helped plenty."

Chance pulled off his hat and wiped his forehead. "You're as stubborn as your dad. I seem to remember when you played good neighbor and helped clean up Joy's house before we brought our baby home from the hospital."

"There were a lot of other church ladies there, too. Besides, Joy is your wife."

Chance arched an eyebrow. "She wasn't then. She was a stranger here. Come on, Tess. Let us help you. We all owe Ray."

Once again Luke found he was envious of Chance having known Tess all those years. "I can help out, too," he added. "I can feed the stock."

"Yeah, my cuz here is just lying around." Chance slapped him on the back. "Hey, come to think of it, I can use you over at my place. I've got several stalls that need to be mucked out."

"Sorry, I'm busy," Luke answered.

"Oh, yeah, you're having about thirty people over tonight." He leaned forward. "The Meyers family is invited, too."

Tess looked at both men in surprise.

"It's just a little Randell get together," Luke told her. "It seems I'm being welcomed back into the family."

Four hours later Luke had watched as truckloads of Randells arrived at the Rocking R. Every family member, either by blood or adoption, had come to see him. They'd set up tables and chairs in the shaded yard. The Randell women worked efficiently together, organizing the food while six brothers supervised the lighting of the barbecue grill. The children, fifteen altogether, looked after each other, with the older ones in charge.

Hank Barrett was the family patriarch. It was obvious that Jack's sons, Chance, Cade and Travis, loved and respected the man, as did their wives, Joy, Abby and Josie. Josie was Hank's biological daughter, whom he hadn't found until she was an adult and came here looking for him.

What a crazy family; and Luke envied his cousins even more because they'd had Hank to bring them up, after their father, Jack Randell, deserted them.

"It's a little overwhelming," Hank said as he came up beside him.

"The noise takes a little getting used to."

A big grin appeared on the old rancher's face. "It's great." He took a drink from his long-neck bottle. "And I love every minute of it."

Luke turned his attention to the crowd and spotted Tess holding one of the babies. She took great care to support the infant's head as she showed him off to Livy.

"That's Chance's boy," Hank commented with a nod. "Jake Michael. I was wondering if he was going to spend his life surrounded by beautiful women. He's still outnumbered by two daughters, Katie and Ellie."

He glanced over at the smiling father. "He doesn't look too unhappy."

"That's because of Joy. A good woman can change a lot of things. Just ask any of my boys. They've been lucky enough to find love."

"Just one big, happy family," Luke murmured as he

continued to watch Tess. A tall, teenage boy came up to her. They seemed engrossed in conversation. The boy's body language told Luke that the kid had more than a passing interest in Tess.

"That's Brandon, Cade's oldest," Hank said. "He didn't get to know his real father until he was nine years old. Cade and Abby were lucky to find their way back to each other. They married and have another son, James Henry, and a little girl, Kristy. Brandon didn't want to leave the ranch, so he goes to college locally.

"Wyatt Gentry came here a few years back to find his father, Jack, but instead he found Maura and her two kids, Jeff and Kelly, living in the old house he'd just bought." Hank took another drink, before he continued the story. "He owns the other part of the Rocking R Ranch. His twin brother, Dylan, an ex-bull rider, came to live there, too. He married Brenna, and they have Sarah Ann and Nicholas. The two brothers raise rough stock for rodeos. They're also part of Mustang Valley Resort and Retreat."

So far Luke had kept up with all the brothers. "So everyone is involved with the Mustang Valley business."

Hank nodded. "Any family member who wants to add to the many services are given consideration." Hank watched him a long time. "You give any more thought to staying?"

"I am staying…for now.

"So you're still planning to sell?"

"I can't do a thing until Brady shows up. I have to say I'm intrigued. I believe that parts of the Rocking R are valuable, especially the strip of land along Mustang Valley."

Hank shrugged. "It would be a shame if the land went to someone outside of the family."

Luke couldn't help but think about it. "Like I said, I'm just hanging out."

"If you get bored let us know, there's plenty to do."

He turned to look at Tess. She was rocking the baby against her breast. She raised her gaze to him, and their eyes locked in a silent gesture that had Luke oblivious to anything else but her.

Hank's voice suddenly broke through his reverie. "She's a special woman."

"Who?"

"Tess. She's special, all right. I've known her since she was Livy's age. You couldn't find anyone as kind and loving. She's had some rough knocks in life, but she's managed to come out of them. It's a shame about Ray."

Luke wanted to ask about Livy's father, but he doubted Hank would say anything. "Yeah, that's rough."

"I'm glad you'll be around for a while. She doesn't ask for help much."

"She doesn't need to ask. Not as long as I'm here."

"That's nice to know, son. That's nice to know."

Twenty minutes later Chance called out that the steaks were ready. Everyone cheered and headed to the tables.

After the blessing everyone began passing food around the long table. Luke quickly realized that it was difficult to carry on a conversation. He sat back and listened mostly. Then he realized that he was the only Randell who wasn't a couple. Even Hank and Ella were together.

Luke had heard the story that Ella had been Hank's

housekeeper for years and helped raise Jack's boys. He finally admitted his feelings for her and they married a few years ago. She officially became Grandma Ella.

Tess glanced across the table at Luke. He looked overwhelmed by the large group, all the questions. She was feeling a little of the same, but she'd been to Randell barbecues before and knew what took place.

It was different for Luke. This was his family. Did he accept that, or was he crazy enough to push them aside and walk away?

"Hey, cuz," a grinning Travis called out. "I hear you're a hotshot real estate developer."

Tess watched Luke tense.

"Not so much anymore. As you might know, the real estate market is in a slump."

Travis called out, "So, does that mean you're going to try your hand at ranching?"

CHAPTER SIX

Six Randell women had invaded his kitchen, but Luke wasn't about to chase them out, not after seeing the row of pies on the counter.

The seventh woman was Hank Barrett's wife, Ella, a handsome older woman dressed in jeans and a plaid shirt. Rumor was she wasn't the best cook in the kitchen, so she organized things and left the preparation to the younger women.

Chance's wife was petite, but she managed to keep up with Cade and Chance's wives, Abby and Josie. As rowdy as the Randell men were, their wives seemed to be able to handle them. That included the half brothers' spouses, Dana Trager, and Maura and Brenna Gentry. They'd all come here to find their roots and found a spot in the Randell family, too. It sent a longing through Luke like he'd never experienced before.

He backed out of the kitchen slowly, not wanting to answer another fifty questions from the women. Outside he found most of the men at the corral. He wandered over to see twelve-year-old Jeff Gentry on Dusty, and

The French Issue

bake
FROM SCRATCH

61

French Recipes You Can Make at Home

The Essential
Brioche
(including this chocolate loaf)

FEATURING

French Cookies & Macarons   Easy Gâteaux
The Quest for the Perfect Croissant

Over 60% OFF the cover price

SUBSCRIBE AND SAVE

☐ **1 year (6 issues) for $39.95**
☐ **2 years (12 issues) for $59.95** ← BEST DEAL!

Name _____

Address _____

City _____

State _____ Zip _____

E-mail _____
(Fill in e-mail address to receive the free *Bake from Scratch* newsletter and other updates.)

☐ **Payment enclosed**

☐ **Bill me (U.S. only)**

BFS JBFS1A122

Canada add $10 postage, other countries outside U.S. add $20 postage for each year. Pay in U.S. funds only. Payment must accompany orders from outside U.S. Please allow 4-8 weeks delivery for new subscriptions. AL residents add appropriate sales tax. *Bake from Scratch* is published 6 times a year. Cover price is $12.99.

BFS JBFS1a1122

BUSINESS REPLY MAIL

FIRST-CLASS MAIL   PERMIT NO. 491   BIRMINGHAM AL

POSTAGE WILL BE PAID BY ADDRESSEE

bake
FROM SCRATCH™

P.O. BOX 6201
Harlan, IA 51593-3701

nineteen-year-old Brandon on Whiskey. They were cutting calves from the small herd.

Cheers of encouragement came from the group of spectators perched on the top of the fence. The oldest Randell grandson, Brandon, looked as comfortable in the saddle as if he were in an easy chair. The younger one didn't look bad, either.

"Hey, Luke," Cade called out to him. "You want your turn with the junior group?"

Luke was as competitive as the next guy, but he wasn't about to be bullied into something he wasn't sure he could do. Before he could turn down the offer, Chance spoke up. "Luke worked Dusty this morning with me. I have to say I was impressed by the way he handled him."

"Then I guess we need to sign him up for the Circle B rodeo next month," Cade suggested.

Goodnaturedly the rest of the Randells started pitching to Luke about entering Hank's annual neighborhood Rodeo in a few months. The talking quickly died out when Tess emerged from her house escorting her father.

Hank and Chance went over to greet Ray. He smiled as they all exchanged handshakes. Luke could see that they'd been more than just neighbors over the years; they were friends, too.

Luke watched the touching scene and realized he couldn't name a single one of his neighbors in Dallas. He discovered that the only socializing he'd done had been for business.

Ray spotted him and nodded as he continued to walk in his direction. "Hello, Luke."

"Ray. It's good to see you out."

"I might not be enjoying this day if you hadn't helped Tess the other night."

"Not a problem, sir. I have to practice my riding."

"Well, from what I could see, you handled yourself just fine."

Hank nodded his approval as he guided Ray on toward the corral, but Cade and Chance hung back. "Nice going, cuz," Cade said. "You're okay in my book."

Luke got slaps on the back from both men before they trailed off after Ray and Hank.

Luke felt a strange tightness in his chest. Why had his cousins' remarks meant so much to him?

Tess stayed behind with Luke and they watched Ray's enthusiasm over the cutting competition.

"The doctor started Dad on a new medication," she began. "Along with some vitamin supplements. There's a study program that Dad might qualify for."

He nodded. "It's good to see him outside."

"Hank had a talk with him. He told him he's wasting a lot of good times he could be enjoying with his family and friends."

"Good for Hank."

They stood there for a long time. His mother would have hated this. She wasn't fond of the Randell cousins. Luke couldn't help but think about what he'd missed when his parents moved him away.

There were times since his return that he'd wanted to fit in with the rest of the Randells. Was the Rocking R the place he should be? He glanced at Tess, remembering the kiss they'd shared at the cabin. There was no doubt she'd drawn him in a way no other woman ever had.

But they both had other commitments. Tess had her family to think about, and he had no money…and a sketchy future. Right now everything was on hold, and a relationship was the last thing he needed.

Tess's voice broke through his reverie as they wandered away from the large crowd. "I want Dad to have the best care…. But the thought of putting him in a nursing home kills me.

"If you could have known him before…even a year ago. He rode in the rodeo circuit. That's where he met my mother. They fell in love and were married a few months later. Dad came back to Mom's parents' ranch, and he learned to train cutting and reining horses." She smiled. "Then I came along. I thought life was pretty great until I was about Livy's age, when my mother got sick. She had cancer…and died about a year later."

"I'm sorry."

She sighed as they strolled toward a shady area and away from the noise in the corral. "I did better than Dad," she told him. "He was lost for a long time, until we moved here. He seemed to thrive, working his own place. Dad started running cattle, but he also bred horses— saddle horses back then. But he knew good quality. And he taught me everything I know." She looked at him, her blue eyes sad. "I can't just abandon him."

Luke's stomach knotted. And he might be the bastard who was taking everything away from her. "No one wants you to. Is there any other family?"

"No, just Bernice and Livy. Bernice moved here right after Dad was diagnosed."

"So what were your plans if your father hadn't gotten…sick?"

"Renew the lease on the ranch," she told him. "Whiskey was going to be a NCHA Champion. And we were going breed other cutting horses."

He couldn't help her on the first one. "How long are you able to run this place by yourself?"

She stopped walking when they reached the tree in the yard. "I can't handle the cattle operation without help. For now the Randells are helping out, then I'll sell the herd off after the roundup next month. I can teach riding and help Chance with some horse training." She paused. "Now, if you're planning to stay on and live here permanently, I'd still like to stay on as your foreman…."

"Do you really see me as a cattle rancher?"

She shrugged. "Maybe not, but you have prime acreage along the valley, and that's worth a lot to the other Randells. I'm sure they'd want that strip of land, if only to protect their nature resort…and the mustangs."

He needed to tell her his situation. "To be honest, Tess, I need the money from this place. And that seems to be the best part of the Rocking R. If I were to develop that land—"

She gasped. "You'd build in the valley? But what will happen to the mustangs?"

"I may not have a choice. The ranch is all I have left. And I have to share it with a brother I can't seem to find. I have to do what I can just to survive."

"What if your brother wants to keep the ranch?"

He was so tired of talking about Brady. Seems his

future hinged on what his brother wanted. "I guess you'll have to wait until he gets here. Who knows, maybe you can cozy up to him and work out some sort of deal." The second he said the words and saw Tess's hurt look, he wanted to take them back.

Luke reached for her. "Tess, I'm sorry. I have no right—"

"No, don't." She pulled away and walked off. He started after her but quickly stopped. He didn't want to have this discussion in front of the Randells.

Suddenly there was more commotion up by the house. A late-model black Mercedes parked by the back door, and a tall brunette climbed out. Luke's heart sank, and dread overtook him when he realized it was Gina Chilton. He wanted to disappear, but she'd already spotted him and called out his name.

What the hell was she doing here?

Seemed as if everyone else wanted to know the same thing. She smiled and hurried toward him as fast as she could in high-heeled sandals. He glanced over her cream-colored skirt that hit just above the knees, and a silky, royal-blue T-shirt. Her dark hair was cut in a straight blunt line, just above her shoulders.

Luke waited to feel some kind of emotion as his former business partner's daughter, and his one-time lover approached…but he didn't. He didn't want her here, intruding in his life.

Luke tensed. "What are you doing here—"

Gina stopped his words when her mouth covered his in a kiss.

* * *

Two hours later all the Randells had packed up and gone home, leaving Luke to deal with Gina. He hated being caught off guard, but he was definitely curious about why she showed up unannounced. There had to be a good reason, because Gina never did anything unless it benefited her. That was for damn sure.

And he couldn't wait to hear it.

After her own tour of the house, Gina floated into the kitchen. Her clothes left little to the imagination. She was a man's dream woman. Just not his. These days he was more into women in fitted jeans, T-shirts and dusty boots.

"Oh, Luke. This is a beautiful house. It's so quaint. Of course it needs work, but your mother's antiques are exquisite. And there's a beautiful hand-carved jewelry box…." Her eyes lit up. "I wonder what treasures could be inside?"

Luke ignored her rambling. "After all this time, you're here talking about this house."

"Oh, but this would be a perfect property to turn into a dude ranch."

He ignored her comments. "Why are you really here, Gina?"

She put on her best smile and gave his boots, jeans and Western shirt the once-over. "I missed you, of course." She sauntered up to him. "And I have to admit, I like your new cowboy look."

He wasn't buying it. Actually, he found he was immune to her. "And this visit…it was because all of a sudden you started thinking about me? You didn't have any trouble walking away when daddy called you."

"I thought about you…a lot," she admitted.

He folded his arms over his chest. "Funny, I couldn't seem to find you or Buck four months ago when I was fighting for my financial life."

She looked sad. "We had to get out, too, Luke. Daddy had a lot more to lose in that deal."

"So you both left me to take the loss on everything."

"That's why I came here, to tell you I'm sorry." She slipped her arms around his neck. "And to make it up to you."

Gina's perfectly made-up face suddenly seemed cold and hard. Why hadn't he noticed it before? He decided he preferred the fresh-scrubbed look better. Tess.

He removed her arms and stepped back. "There's no need to, Gina. You've already let me know where you stand."

She pouted. "Don't be that way, Luke. Daddy sent me to help you."

He laughed. "No, thanks. I've had your help before and I can do without it." He wanted her gone. "So please leave."

She looked surprised. "At least hear me out. It's a great deal. You can make up everything and more of what you lost."

Luke was curious. "Okay, talk."

She grew serious. "It's a great property. We can develop it with luxury homes and horse property in a gated community. We can even put in an executive golf course."

Not that he was thinking of partnering with Gina ever again, but he couldn't help but ask, "And where do we get the backing? My reputation and credit is in the toilet."

"That's the best part, sweetheart. You already own the property."

"The Rocking R Ranch."

She smiled. "It's even got a great ring to it, The Rocking R Estates…located in Mustang Valley."

"Mommy, why was that lady kissing Mr. Luke?" Livy asked as she put on her nightgown.

Tess didn't want to know. It was none of her business. "Mr. Luke said she was a friend that he used to work with."

"But Brandon told Jeff she was a hot babe. What does that mean?"

"That means you shouldn't have been listening to other peoples' conversations."

"I didn't mean to. The words just sneaked into my ears. Do you think Miss Gina is going to move into the house with Mr. Luke? I hope not 'cause I don't think she likes little kids." Livy climbed into bed and Tess pulled the covers up.

"Maybe it would be a good idea for you to not go to the house for a while."

"Are you mad at Mr. Luke, Mommy?" her daughter asked.

"No, sweetie. I'm just tired." But she was sad she'd let herself care for a man who ended up hurting her.

After a kiss on her daughter's cheek, Tess left the bedroom and walked out to the living room where Bernice was watching television.

"I'm going to check on the horses," she called as she walked out the back door.

She needed the solitude of the lone walk, hoping to

clear her head of the sight of that woman kissing Luke. She hated that she cared, but she refused to look toward the house to see if Gina Chilton's car was still there.

She'd been such a fool to think that Luke Randell might want to fit in here. That he might stay and let her continue the lease agreement. Any hope of that, and her dream of breeding horses, was dimming quickly.

She stepped inside the barn and started down the aisle illuminated by soft light. After the amount of exercise the horses received today, she didn't expect any of them to be restless. The stalls were quiet, but she still wanted to check Whiskey.

The stallion raised his head over the gate and greeted her. "Hey, fella, had a lot of fun today, didn't you?"

The animal bobbed his head and nuzzled her for more attention. "You're just like all men, can't get enough." She smiled, but it faded quickly.

Was Gina the woman in Luke's life? Would she take him back to Dallas? Tess shook away any thoughts of the man. She wasn't going to waste her time.

"Tess…"

She glanced up to see Luke standing in the aisle. He had on his jeans, but his shirt was unbuttoned and pulled from the waistband. His hair was mussed as if his fingers combed though it…or someone else had. "Bernice said you came out here. Is everything okay?"

"It's perfect." She turned away and paid attention to Whiskey. "Just checking on the horses. What are you doing here? Don't you have a houseguest?"

He walked to her. "I don't have any guests, invited or otherwise. And Gina wasn't invited."

"It's not my concern who your friends are." She grabbed the halter off the gate and walked off.

Luke was tired of stubborn females, this one especially. He went after her, following her into the tack room. "Well, I need you to hear me out about Gina."

"I don't need to hear anything," she told him, hanging the halter on a hook.

"Too bad, you're going to listen," he said. "I didn't invite Gina, nor did I know she was coming here. I never expected to see her again."

"Well, she seemed to think that you'd welcome her with open arms."

Luke was tickled that Tess cared that much. "At one time I would have…but not anymore. She knows that now, and she's headed back to Dallas."

Tess paused, then murmured, "It matters if she took your heart with her."

Luke didn't want Tess to think Gina was still part of his life. "Looking back…I think Gina bruised my pride and destroyed my ego, but my heart…not so much." He moved closer to the woman who had gotten his attention. "I guess I wanted something so badly. I started fantasizing about a perfect life. Now, I think Gina and I used each other and it cost me…a lot."

Tess looked at him. Her gaze locked with his, and he had to fight not to take her in his arms. "I think I'm starting to realize I want something different now."

There was another long pause. "What about you, Tess Meyers? One man broke your heart, so you keep us all at arm's length?"

She swallowed. "I have too much at stake to have a casual relationship. Livy being the most important reason."

He couldn't help but be curious. "Has her father ever been in her life?"

She shook her head. "He had another family he'd conveniently neglected to tell me about." She stole a glance at him. "I was just a naive college student who fell for her married professor. Although at twenty-two, I should have known better. Believe me, I wised up quickly. After Livy was born, I had him sign away all rights to his daughter."

Luke cursed, then suddenly reached for Tess, taking her in his arms. "Good riddance," he whispered, closing his eyes at the incredible feeling of her body pressed against his. He felt her tremble, or maybe it was him. "You deserve so much more, Tess. Livy deserves more." He drew back and looked at her. "You're a beautiful woman." He couldn't let her go. "There's a man out there who would love you and your child."

Tess didn't believe in pretty words anymore. "Yeah, they're just pounding down my door." She managed a weak smile. "I'm not looking, Luke. All I want is to make a good living for my family."

And yet, she wanted to bury deeper into Luke's embrace. Just for a little while she wanted someone who would take away her burden…tell her everything would be okay. She was scared to let herself trust again. To fall in love…

She stopped herself. No. She couldn't let that happen. Not with a man who would leave. She moved away. "I stopped believing in fairy tales a long time ago."

He arched an eyebrow and showed off a slow, sexy smile. "Are you so sure Prince Charming isn't out there?"

She frowned, wishing she could be as lighthearted about it as he was. "Like I said, I'm not looking."

He leaned forward. "I think you're afraid, Tess Meyers."

"I'm practical," she argued.

"And stubborn."

He moved toward her and she didn't back away, telling herself it was because the room was small.

His head lowered to hers. "And beautiful…and far too tempting."

Tess gave a weak protest, but it died quickly when his mouth covered hers in a soft kiss. He pulled back and she silently begged for more. He didn't disappoint as he wrapped his arms around her, pulling her tight against him, and closed his mouth over hers again.

She released a soft moan as her hands slid up his chest and around his neck as he deepened the kiss. He teased the seam of her lips until she gave him access, then his tongue moved inside, stroking against hers until she made a whimpering sound.

Finally Luke broke off the kiss, but didn't release her. His heated gaze locked on hers. "I need to add *dangerous* to the list."

"Then maybe we shouldn't do this again," she said weakly.

"Yeah, right," he breathed as his head came down and captured her mouth again. His hand caressed her back as he drew her against his hard body. She could feel his desire, but even that didn't frighten her. She wanted Luke Randell.

By the time he released her, he looked as stunned as she felt. "Damn, woman, you make me forget everything…and want everything." His hands cupped her face, his gaze searching hers. "I want you," he confessed, right before his mouth crushed against hers. The kiss was hungry and needy, for both of them.

Somehow Luke managed to push her backward until her legs bumped against the edge of the cot. He drew her down until her head met the wool blanket. Tess opened her eyes to protest against going any further, but when her gaze locked with Luke's her desire soared to new heights.

Luke pulled her shirt from her jeans and put his hands on her bare skin. "Silk," he breathed. He leaned down and kissed her, then trailed his mouth along her jaw, her neck to her breasts.

She gasped, and clutched at his head. "Oh, Luke," she whispered.

He looked at her. "You feel it, too. That happens when we're together. You drive me crazy. I want you so much. Tell me you feel the same."

Tess pushed all caution aside. She wanted Luke, too, if only for a short time. She raised up and placed her mouth against his. "Yes…I want you," she whispered.

He pulled her tight against him as she arched into the kiss, not wanting to lose any contact. Before their passion could be satisfied, his cell phone rang.

He broke off the kiss, but didn't move away.

"You better answer that," she told him.

Finally he pulled the phone from his pocket and

stood. Tess tugged her shirt down and drew a calming breath. Her hands were shaking, realizing how far…and how lost she was in Luke's arms.

"This is Luke Randell." He paused and listened. "Yes, Brady Randell is my brother." A long pause as his eyes narrowed. "How bad?"

Tess sat on the edge of the bunk when Luke flipped close his phone. "Well, it looks like I finally get to meet my brother that is, if he survives long enough for me to get to him."

CHAPTER SEVEN

THE next twenty-four hours passed in a blur for Luke.

The call from Brady's commanding officer hadn't divulged much information, only that his brother's plane had crashed during a mission. Brady had to eject from his F-16, but not without injuries. It was touch-and-go for a while, but Brady had survived twenty-four hours before he'd been located, then he'd been taken to Ramstein Base in Germany, then to the second army hospital at Landstuhl. Although he was still critical he was flown home to the States.

It had been Tess who'd taken over and made the necessary calls. The first one to Chance. An hour later Chance and Cade had picked him up and driven him to the airport, but instead of dropping him off, they'd boarded the plane with him.

Luke wasn't used to having this kind of support. He'd been on his own most of his life, but there hadn't been any doubt that both cousins were accompanying him to Walter Reed Hospital in Washington, D.C.

Once they arrived at the hospital, Chance talked

with the nurse on duty at the desk. It seemed to take forever, but Luke needed time to gather his thoughts and his emotions.

He might not have liked that Brady had been the son who had a life with their father, but he'd never wanted anything bad to happen to him. And this could be bad. No matter the circumstances, Brady was his brother.

Suddenly that mattered to him.

His cousins walked back to the waiting area. "The nurse is going to get the doctor on the case."

Luke sat down as his thoughts turned to Tess and how she'd been there for him. She'd made him call back Brady's commanding officer to get more information. When Luke was reluctant to make the trip, Tess told him he couldn't ignore the fact he had a brother. And if he didn't go to see Brady, he'd be sorry.

Luke took a breath and released it. Just months ago his life was less complicated—no family, no financial problems. No Tess. His life had been pretty lonely. He felt a strange tightening in his gut. Not anymore.

Chance and Cade stood as the doctor approached. "Mr. Randell?"

"I'm Luke Randell," he said. "These men are my cousins, Chance and Cade Randell.

"I'm Dr. Newberry." They all shook hands. "I'm handling Captain Brady's case. I'm sure your brother will be happy his family is here."

Luke had to ask the dreaded question, "How is my brother, Doctor?"

"He had several injuries, including some internal bleeding, but the surgeons at Landstuhl Hospital got it under control. Also, after he ejected from his plane his leg was shattered on the landing. That, combined with Captain Randell having been exposed to the elements overnight before he was rescued, made his condition more serious."

"How is he now?"

"He's been upgraded to stable. He's still heavily sedated. The surgeons operated on his leg this morning, but that's only the beginning of his recovery. There could be more surgeries, and a lot of therapy to bring his leg back to normal."

Luke swallowed, surprised at the feelings churning through him. "But he's going to be okay?"

The doctor sighed. "He's strong. And barring any complications, he'll survive…but I can't guarantee he'll be able to fly again."

With that announcement, Dr. Newberry took them to the elevator, and they rode up to recovery. "Just one visitor at a time and keep it short."

Luke followed the doctor to the doorway of Brady's room, but he didn't go in right away. He just stood outside and stared at the man lying in the bed. His left leg was elevated as machines monitored his vital signs. A white sheet covered his brother's large frame. A shock of nearly black hair was cut military short. His face was shadowed by a dark beard.

Cade and Chance came up on either side of Luke. "Hey, this is a tough way to meet your brother for the first time," Cade said. "If you'd rather wait…"

"No, I've waited long enough. As you would say, it's time to cowboy up." He stepped through the door. The sounds of the monitor beeping seemed to keep rhythm with the heavy pounding of his own heart.

He walked toward the side of the bed. The stranger lying there had scratches and bruises on his face. A face that strikingly resembled his father's. Luke blew out a breath, trying to slow his pulse. Damn, this was hard.

Chance appeared beside him. "You okay?"

Luke nodded. "I'm not sure what to do."

"You're here," his cousin said. "You two are family. You have to take the good with the bad. He's a Randell, too, and we don't do things the easy way." Chance gave him a half smile. "I'll be just outside if you need me."

Once again Luke was alone. He'd never realized how often he'd faced things solo until he'd spent a good part of the past week with the Randells. And Tess. Now…his brother.

A groan came from the man in the bed as he started shifting around.

Luke was afraid he would hurt himself. "Hey, I think you're supposed to lie still."

The patient opened his eyes, and after a few blinks, Brady's dark gaze glared back at him. "Who the hell are you?"

"Luke…Randell." He motioned over his shoulder. "Those two guys are our cousins, Chance and Cade Randell."

Brady continued to frown. "If you're here to claim the body, you'll have to wait, I'm not dead yet."

Later that evening, after a long bedtime story, Tess finally got Livy to sleep. She checked in on her father to see that he was down for the night, too. He was exhausted after spending his first day at the seniors' center. They had an exercise program for Alzheimer's patients. Whether the new medication and exercise was helping slow down the disease, only time would only tell. Precious time that could possibly give Ray Meyers the best quality of life. And for her to have her dad with her a little longer.

She went into the kitchen to find Bernice drinking a cup of tea.

"Everyone asleep?"

Tess nodded. "That's what I should be doing, too." She yawned but knew sleep wouldn't come easy, especially not knowing what was going on with Luke.

"He probably can't call you," Bernice said.

It was foolish to act as if she didn't know who her aunt was talking about. "I don't expect a call. Luke's with his brother."

"You could call Chance's wife."

"No, it's too late," Tess told her as she glanced at the clock. "And if there were any news, we'd hear."

The sound of the ringing phone caused her to jump. Tess went to answer it. "Hello."

"Tess," Luke said, his voice was husky.

"Luke." She felt her heart drumming in her chest.

"I'm sorry to call so late."

"No, it's not too late," she told him as a smiling Bernice walked out of the kitchen. "Luke, is everything all right?"

"Better than I first thought. Brady has some serious injuries, but none life threatening. And he's not exactly crazy to see me here."

"He's probably in a lot of pain. Are you going to stay there?"

There was a long pause. "Why, do you miss me?"

Her breath caught. She was afraid to say too much. "Livy wants you to come back."

Another pregnant pause. "Not that I don't care about shortcake, but I want to know about her mother. Tess, do you want me to come back?"

Inside she wanted to take a risk with him. But in the end she could get hurt when he left. "Luke…this isn't wise for either one of us. We have too many other things to deal with."

"I know this isn't the right time. But I keep wishing you were here with me." She could hear the emotion in his voice. "Thank you for talking me into coming."

"Family's important."

He sighed. "I'm beginning to believe that."

The next morning Luke, Chance and Cade headed back to the hospital. He'd only gotten a few hours of sleep after talking with Tess. He knew they shouldn't get involved, but that hadn't stopped his feelings for her. It was the wrong time to think about complicating his life with a relationship…with a woman and a child. He wasn't able to offer her any sort of future.

Luke stopped at the nurses' desk to learn his brother had been moved into a four-man ward. Cade and Chance waited outside while Luke went in.

He found Brady in the bed next to the window. He looked a little better today, but he could see the pain etched around his eyes.

"Morning, Brady," he said.

His brother grimaced as he shifted in the bed. "You still here?"

"I said I'd be back," Luke told him. "I wanted to make sure you're okay."

"Yeah, I'm just great."

"The doctor said you were lucky. You could have died out there." Luke shrugged. "Wherever there is."

"I was on a mission. The destination isn't important. And they got me out." Brady studied him. "I heard you've been looking for me for a while. I didn't have you on my emergency contact list."

"I called your commanding officer last week. Weren't you notified about Sam's will?"

"I was there when Dad's will was read." His gaze narrowed. "Too bad you couldn't even take the time to show up at the funeral."

Luke stiffened. "I wasn't invited."

"You were invited to a lot of things, you just couldn't find the time to come around. I guess Dad finally stopped asking."

"Asking? Sam Randell walked out one day and never came back. He made the choice not to be in my life. His career and his new family didn't leave any room for me." Luke had told himself he wasn't going to rehash this old topic. "Okay, let's just put it in the past and move on. I came here to see how you were, but there's a lot of unfinished business. Our father left us the Rocking R Ranch."

"I know," Brady said. "Dad told me a while ago."

Luke fought his anger. "In a little over a month Ray

Meyers's lease will end. We have to decide if we're going to renew or sell…"

Brady shook his head. "I've already decided," he said. "I'm not selling."

Luke tensed. "Then I guess we'll need to get a lawyer because I can't afford to keep the land. It's more valuable to me if it's developed."

"Out for the almighty dollar, huh, bro?"

"I'm out to survive," Luke countered. "But if you want to buy me out, you're more than welcome. But just be aware, family or no family, I'm not going to give the land away."

Later that evening Luke pulled a beer out of the refrigerator. They'd left Washington that afternoon and arrived home about nine o'clock. That pleased Luke, since he didn't want to see anyone. He had too much thinking to do.

How was he going to manage much longer? He had to come up with something. After he'd talked to his accountant that morning, he discovered that after he'd made financial restitution to all parties involved in the bad real estate deal, he had little left in the bank. He'd been poor before, during the years his mother had to work to support them.

But it was harder to swallow now. He'd worked relentlessly over the years to build financial stability. Six months ago he'd owned a lot of possessions. Maybe he'd been too greedy.

Achieving financial success had been everything in his life. Nothing else had seemed to matter. Now, after just a short time here, he wasn't sure of anything except he and his new brother were already in for a fight.

In the moonlight Tess walked across the yard to the large house. It probably wasn't wise to go and see Luke, but she told herself she was just curious about how things went with Brady.

She glanced down at the T-shirt and cotton skirt she'd changed into after her shower. So what if she wanted to look nice? The one thing she couldn't deny was she and Luke had nearly made love the last time they were together. To get involved with Luke would be a mistake, but she couldn't make herself turn around and run back to her house.

Instead she looked up and saw Luke walk out onto the porch. Her heart began to pound like a galloping horse as she took in his large frame silhouetted in the moonlight—those broad shoulders and a torso that tapered down into a narrow waist. He wore jeans and boots as well as any rancher who was born to the life.

He raised a long-neck beer bottle and took a long drink. He looked tired. Her palms itched with the desire to comfort him.

Suddenly he looked in her direction. "Tess…"

"Hi, Luke," she said as she came closer. "I just wanted to make sure you got back okay."

Luke forced a smile. He was still numb from his trip, but seeing Tess brought back his enthusiasm…and stirred a lot of feelings. "I'm a little tired, but I'm good. Chance and Cade made sure of that. They're more like nursemaids than cousins."

"I'm glad they went with you." She climbed the steps and stood in front of him. The light from the kitchen showed off her soft skin and incredible eyes. Her blond hair curled against her shoulders. The way he liked it. Touchable.

"We couldn't do much but wait around." He remembered the last time he'd seen Tess her mouth was swollen from his kisses, her body was responding to his touch.

He quickly shook away the wayward direction of his thoughts.

"What about you?" she asked in a soft voice. "How do you feel after meeting your brother after all this time?"

"It's strange." He couldn't stop staring at her. He took a step closer. "But I don't want to talk about Brady. I'm glad you came by." He drew her into his arms. "You have no idea how much I've missed you…" Before she could protest, his mouth covered hers.

He felt her hands move upward around his neck. A whimper escaped as he deepened the kiss. By the time he released her, he wanted to carry her upstairs to his bed.

"You feel so good." He kissed her again and again. His hand cupping her breast through her shirt. "All I could think about was what nearly happened between us in the barn."

She looked at him, her own hunger and need showing in her eyes, but she slowly slipped from his arms. "And maybe it's a good thing nothing had happened," she said. "We shouldn't go any further."

He stared at her. She was right, but that didn't stop

how he was starting to feel toward her. But she'd hate him for what he needed to do—to sell out to the highest bidder. "You're right, Tess. You deserve more."

"No, Luke, it's not that. We're both at a time in our lives where neither one of us needs more complications. I need to keep my focus on building a future for my family."

Something inside him wanted to argue, but she was speaking the truth. "And that's what you should do."

Suddenly she smiled at him. "And I did. What I really came to tell you is I entered Whiskey in the San Angelo Rodeo this weekend."

He couldn't help but grin, too. "How about that? So you're on your way."

"Well, we haven't won anything yet."

"You will," he encouraged. "You're so good at what you do, and you've got a great horse."

"We'll see," she said, then hesitated. "I guess I'd better get back to the house." Again she hesitated. "Good night, Luke."

He couldn't let her go, not yet.

When she started to turn away, he reached for her and his mouth came down on hers. His arms circled her waist and brought her against him. He could feel every subtle curve, her heat as her body arched into him. His hands moved to her face, cupping her cheeks as he deepened the kiss. A kiss he never wanted to end. But he knew he was just delaying the inevitable, and he had to let her go.

With the last of his strength, he backed away. His eyes met hers, unable to miss the passion in their depths.

Before he could change his mind, he turned and walked inside, praying she wouldn't call him back.

In the end he was disappointed that she didn't.

A week later Luke arrived at the crowded First Community Credit Union Spur Arena in San Angelo. Chance had wanted to see how Whiskey performed and had invited him along. Luke told himself it was to spend time with his cousins, but he, too, was curious to see Tess.

"Hey, there's Hank," Chance said as they walked past the row of pens until they reached the rows of bleachers in the arena. After climbing up several levels, they found where Hank, Travis and Cade were seated together.

Hank greeted him with a handshake. "Luke, nice to see you."

"Good to see you, too."

Luke sat down beside the older man. An air of excitement filled the huge arena as people mingled around looking for seats. Luke glanced toward the numerous pens filled with stock for the rodeo. Colorful banners hung from the rafters, and music mixed with the voices of excited fans.

His thoughts turned to Tess. No doubt she was nervous. Whiskey was a big key to her future. He'd stayed away from her this week, knowing it was for the best, although, he could see her in the corral from the bedroom window as she'd worked with Whiskey.

Chance had stopped by a few times, giving her advice on the training. Luke hated the fact that seeing the two together made him jealous. Not that he thought anything was going on between them. Chance was crazy about his wife. Luke wished he could be the one to help Tess.

He'd always run from women like Tess Meyers—the type who wanted a permanent relationship. That's what he enjoyed about Gina. She was a user, just like he was.

Tess wasn't capable of using anyone. She was honest, independent and…loving. Everything Luke Randell wasn't. He needed to stay away…but yet, here he was.

"Hey, Mr. Luke." Livy's voice broke into his thoughts.

Luke couldn't help but smile, seeing the miniature version of Tess dressed in her jeans, boots and a bright-pink Western shirt. "Well, look who's here."

The child's smile brightened. "My mommy is riding Whiskey in the show. Aunt Bernie and me are gonna cheer for them. Are you gonna, too?"

"You bet." He pulled her into a hug, realizing how much he'd missed her not being around this past week. "I'm going to cheer really loud."

"And she's gonna win. Mr. Chance said so."

Luke glanced toward his cousin and realized that he wasn't in his seat. "Well, Chance should know, huh?"

"You know what else? I'm going to spend the night with Katie and Ellie 'cause I start school next week. It's a girl night, we're going to do makeup and stuff." Those eyes widened. "I never done that, but Mommy says I'm old enough now." She shook her head, causing her ponytail to swing around. "But it's only cause it's a special 'casion."

"Sounds like you're going to have fun."

Bernice arrived and sat on the row of bleachers just below him. "Livy, give Luke a chance to breathe," she said.

"But I need to tell him a lot of stuff."

"Well, save some for later, he'll be here awhile."

"Okay." The child climbed down to her seat.

"Looks like you've got the attention of a pretty little lady," Hank said.

Luke shrugged. "Livy visits me sometimes," he said, enjoying the child's presence. Strange, for someone who didn't like to keep anyone too close, he suddenly had gotten attached to a lot of people.

"It's kind of hard not to take notice of those lovely lady neighbors."

"Tess carries a heavy load."

Hank nodded. "Yeah, she does. I'm glad you're around to help out. But that's what Texas neighbors do. They look after one another. It's good that you and your brother are coming back home."

"Whoa…I'm not sure what Brady's plans are, but I can't stay. I'm not a rancher, Hank, so I have to find a way to make a living."

Hank frowned. "Maybe there's a way you could do both."

Before Luke could ask Hank what he was talking about, the announcer came on and had everyone stand. He stood and watched the women on horseback, carrying the American and Texas flags around the arena, then stopped in the center while the crowd sang the National Anthem.

After about ten minutes of announcements, they started the first session, the cutting competition. He quickly turned his attention to the pens and finally located the beautiful bay stallion being led by Tess. She was dressed in a bright-blue Western blouse and dark jeans, and caramel-colored chaps. Her hair was tied back in a ponytail with a black Stetson tugged low on her head.

She was busy talking with Chance, and it looked like he was giving her some last-minute instructions. Suddenly Tess turned toward the bleachers and smiled and waved. His chest tightened, but then he realized she was waving at Livy. He didn't care, he waved back. It was important to him that she know he was here to support her.

When Tess's turn came, she mounted Whiskey. After she was announced, Luke's stomach tightened with nerves as she rode the horse out into the arena.

She looked confident as the competition began and Whiskey went to work. The crowd cheered the duo on as Tess sat in the saddle, the reins slack, her hands on the horn, letting the animal do his job. By the time the two and a half minutes ran out and the buzzer went off, three steers had been cut from the herd.

Luke stuck his fingers in his mouth and let go of a long whistle. Several of the other Randells did the same. Then the score of 74 came up on the board and the crowd roared. Smiling, Tess waved to everyone. He waved back, wondering if she saw him, but he was going to make sure she knew how proud he was of her.

"Come on, Livy. You want to go down and see your mom?"

She cheered. "Can I go, Aunt Bernie?"

"Sure," Bernice said, looking at Luke. "Give her a hug for me."

Holding Livy's tiny hand, he led the way down the steps and along the metal railing until they reached the pen area. That's where they found Tess. When she spotted them, she handed Chance Whiskey's reins and hurried toward them.

"Mommy! You won," Livy called.

"Oh, sweetie, I haven't won yet," she said, then looked at Luke. "Hi."

"Tess, you were great," he told her.

"I think Whiskey deserves some credit, too. Besides, it's only the $3,000 novice division."

"I have a feeling it's just the beginning."

Luke wanted so badly to take her into his arms. And when the last score came up and her name and horse were announced the winner, he got his chance. He reached for her and pulled her into his arms.

"I told you," he whispered, realizing it had been a hell of a long week without her. "You're a winner, Tess."

CHAPTER EIGHT

BEING in Luke's arms, Tess lost all sense of where she was. Until Livy tugged on her arm.

"Hey, Mommy. Is Mr. Luke going to kiss you?"

Tess felt heat rush to her cheeks. What was wrong with her, acting like a teenager.

She quickly pulled away. "Oh, honey, he's just happy I won." She bent down. "But I want a kiss from you."

Her daughter threw her tiny arms around her in a tight embrace and placed a kiss on her cheek. "I love you, Mommy."

"I love you, too, sweetie." She stole a glance at Luke. The good-looking Randell had somehow worked his way into her heart, too. Worse, she didn't seem to know how to stop caring about him.

It wasn't long before her aunt appeared and embraced her. "Oh, honey, Ray's going to be so proud," she said.

Her dad. This was their dream. She wanted him to be here so badly, but she knew it would be too much for him. "As soon as I get Whiskey settled, I'll call him."

"He'd like that."

Tess frowned. "You need me to come home tonight?"

"Oh, no. You have to compete tomorrow." Bernice sent a glance toward Luke. "You stay like you planned and enjoy your victory. You've got your reservations at the hotel. Ray and I will be fine, and Chance is taking Livy to the sleepover with Ellie and Katie."

Livy tugged on her arm. "Don't forget Kelly and Sarah Ann are going to be there, too. And Grandma Ella is going to help watch us."

Tess knew her daughter was excited. This was her first sleepover, and first time away from home. "You sure you don't want me to take you?"

Livy pouted. "Mommy, I'm five. I'm not a baby."

That made Tess a little sad. "Okay, you can go with Chance." After another kiss, her daughter took off with Bernice to find Chance and Hank.

"Don't look so sad," Luke began, "she'll be home tomorrow, wanting to tell you all about it."

"It's her first time away from home." She continued to watch her daughter until she was out of sight. "And her first day of school starts on Tuesday." She took Whiskey's reins and led him down the series of pens, Luke beside her. "I guess I've taken it for granted that she'll always be a baby."

Luke didn't want to leave her. "Kids grow up."

"I know, and she needs me less and less."

"That's because you've raised your daughter to be independent. But Livy will never stop needing you. You're her mother."

They reached the stall area. "Yeah, I am. Oh, boy. If I'm this bad now, how will I act when she goes on her first date? Off to college?" She took Whiskey inside and began to remove his saddle. It was busy work to try to keep her nervousness at bay. Why was Luke hanging around?

Luke knew he should leave, but he couldn't seem to. He looked at Tess, and feelings of possessiveness hit hard. He wasn't going anywhere.

He took the saddle from her and placed it on the stand outside the stall. "What are your plans for tonight?"

"I'm babysitting a horse and catching a few hours' sleep at the motel. Why are you so interested?"

He shrugged. "I was wondering if you could take a break and go to dinner with me?"

Luke drove Tess to a steakhouse not far from the arena. It wasn't the kind of place he normally took a date, but neither one of them were dressed for fine dining.

"The food here is pretty good," Tess said as the waitress walked away with their order. "You didn't need to take me out."

He stared at her. "I wanted to spend time with you, Tess. And I bet it's not often you get out by yourself."

Those blue eyes locked with his. "It's the country, Luke. We get up early and go to bed early, so we don't go out much." She took a sip of water. "I know that's different from what you were used to in Dallas."

He shrugged. "That's not true, I spent a lot of evenings at home. Most of my socializing was for business."

"Did you socialize a lot with Gina?"

He wanted to be honest with her. "Yes. We met through her father, and we were involved in a project together. For a while we were a couple. But I hadn't seen Gina in months...until she showed up at the ranch."

"She must still have feelings for you if she came here…."

He sighed. "Gina was here because of her father. She and Buck have a new deal in the works and she wanted to know if I was interested in investing."

He paused when the waitress brought their iced tea.

"Well, are you? Interested in investing?"

"Honestly, I'm not sure. I can't deny I would like to make some money. I lost everything just six months ago. That doesn't sit right with me. But it's hard to jump into a project when I have a limited cash flow."

"You act like you're destitute. You own half of a cattle ranch." She smiled. "And a beautiful house filled with antiques."

He was crazy about her smile. He also liked having her all to himself, even if it was just for a short time. "What is it with everyone and old furniture?"

She leaned closer. "For one thing, the craftsmanship a hundred years ago was so much better. And for another thing, good pieces are worth a sizable amount of money."

"I'll try to remember that when I'm looking to pay for my next meal." He needed to think seriously about what he was going to do.

She tossed her head back and laughed. "I doubt you'll ever go hungry. Besides, Bernice would never let you skip a meal."

He couldn't stop staring at her. It wasn't just her beauty that drew him, but the way she touched people… took care of her family, and her animals. And he was comfortable being with Tess. He didn't feel any pressure to try and impress her all the time, although he wanted to. He couldn't remember the last time he could just let everything go, and enjoy himself.

From the first, something inside them had connected, and he wanted more than anything to see where this led.

"I enjoy being with you, Tess," he blurted out.

"I like being with you, too," she admitted, then hesitated. "But I don't have much extra time for things like this. My life is pretty full."

"Yet, we somehow manage to find time to end up together."

She glanced away. "But when your brother comes here, you'll be busy, too." She sat back. "Besides you said so yourself you aren't staying."

"I'm not going anywhere right now." He grasped her hand. "Be truthful, Tess. Would you rather have me stick around?"

"What does it matter?" She looked at him. "Unless you've changed your mind about selling…"

"I can't make a move without Brady's input," he said. "Besides, as much as I've tried to keep my distance, I can't seem to manage that, either. For the past week I nearly went crazy being away from you…. I might not be the best bet right now, but I care about you, Tess, a lot."

She sighed but didn't look away. "I'm not any good at this, Luke. Every time I've trusted my feelings…it hasn't worked out."

His hand squeezed hers. He didn't want to mess this up. "Tess, I'd never intentionally hurt you."

"But what if after those few months are up, you get tired of the simple country life? What if I'm not enough?"

"You are more than enough, and any man would be

lucky to have you," he told her, wondering if he would measure up. But he couldn't seem to walk away from her. "Can't we take this one step at a time?"

Before she could give him an answer, the waitress brought their food to the table. The huge steaks didn't look the least bit appetizing.

He found his hunger was for something entirely different than food.

Tess had returned to the arena to make sure Whiskey was settled in for the night. She'd called Bernice to check on Dad and to see if Livy was settled at the party. She turned around and found Luke standing beside the pen. He looked sexy in his Western shirt and creased jeans and spit-shined boots.

She tried to draw air into her lungs, but it was hard. "I guess I'm finished for tonight." She had trouble making eye contact, feeling the electricity sparking between them. "I better get some sleep."

"Sounds like a good idea." He walked alongside her until they reached the door to the parking lot and her truck. "Well, thank you for—"

He stopped her words as he pulled her into his arms and kissed her. By the time he released her, she swayed before she was able to regain her balance.

"No, thank you." He grinned. "I'll follow you to the motel…to make sure you get there safely."

She could only nod as he opened the door to her truck and she slid inside. Trying to slow her heart rate, she watched as he walked to his car.

She was in big trouble.

Ten minutes later Tess pulled into the spot in front of her room. Luke parked a little further away but made it to the door before her. They exchanged a knowing look, and Luke leaned down and brushed a kiss against her lips. Tess knew she wouldn't send him away…not tonight.

With shaky hands Tess managed to work the key card, praying she wasn't making a mistake. She opened the door to the standard-style motel room and walked in. With a bad case of nerves, Tess grabbed the plastic ice bucket.

"I'll get some ice," she said, and he reached for her hand. She froze, suddenly feeling the electrifying heat of his touch.

"We don't need ice, Tess," he said, tossing the bucket aside. "I don't think it's going to help cool us off." He stepped closer and dipped his head to hers.

Tess quickly lost herself in his kiss as his fingers threaded through her hair. She moved closer as his hands worked their way down her spine. She wound her arms around his neck and snuggled against his body, feeling the outline of his desire.

She moaned as he lifted her, angling her hips against his, applying sweet pressure while he deepened the kiss. It was never like this before. She'd never felt this kind of hunger.

He pulled back and sucked in a breath. "Tess. I can't get enough of you." He anchored his hands to the base of her head and tipped it back.

"I want you," he murmured as he trailed soft kisses across her jaw to her ear. "So you'd better throw me out now if you don't want the same thing."

He paused as his eyes searched hers, waiting for her answer.

Her heart was pounding hard. Even with her doubts, she couldn't let him go. "Oh, Luke. I want you, too."

Luke worked the buttons on her blouse, then stripped it off her shoulders. She gasped when his hands brushed against her skin. He ran his fingers over the lacy edge of her bra, then underneath until his palm pressed against her nipple.

She felt her knees go weak but Luke held her tight. He stroked her sensitized skin and all she could do was let herself feel. By the time Luke laid her on the bed, she surrendered to the passion, and to loving this man.

The sun peeked through the edge of the curtain, shining into Tess's eyes. She gasped and sat up in bed, trying to clear her head of sleep.

Where was she?

She glanced down at her naked body, and her memory slowly returned. She'd spent the night making love with Luke. She glanced around the empty room. He was gone. He'd left without saying goodbye?

Hurt took over as she stood and walked to the chair where her clothes were draped over the back.

So was Luke's shirt.

She picked it up, and slipped it on, catching his familiar essence. She closed her eyes, remembering last night and the man who'd made love to her so tenderly that it brought tears to her eyes. She'd never experienced passion like that with another man.

Suddenly the door opened and Luke walked inside dressed in a white T-shirt and jeans and a sexy smile.

"Man, you look good." He was juggling coffee and muffins. "Good morning." He came toward her and leaned down to place a kiss on her surprised lips. "Thought we should grab some food before we head back to the arena."

Tess tried to hide her awkwardness. "You went for breakfast?"

"Yeah, they have a complimentary continental breakfast for the guests." He set the food on the table and turned back to her. "I knew you wanted to get back to Whiskey early." He pulled her into his arms. "But seeing you looking so sexy in my shirt…I may have to delay the trip."

She felt the heat from his body and the familiar touch of his hands. It would be so easy to let him distract her. She tried to pull away. "I really need to get back to the arena."

Luke refused to let her. "Is this about the competition or what happened between us last night?"

She inhaled and moved away from his intoxicating scent. "I have to stay focused on the ride, Luke. That's why I came here."

He frowned. "And I wasn't invited?"

"No! It's just that—" she brushed back her wild hair, hugging the shirt against her body "—I don't exactly know how to handle this…situation."

Luke wasn't sure he knew, either. He only knew that he didn't want it to end with her. "Last night meant a lot to me, Tess. I'm not going to walk away from you. I've tried, but you keep drawing me back."

"I don't try to."

He smiled. "I know. I almost wish you would." He wondered if she needed him like he needed her. "I want to spend time with you."

"But—"

"I know there's a lot of buts. The ranch and my going back to Dallas and my brother, your father, your daughter…" He hugged her close. "God, Tess. There will always be something. But right now I just want to hang on to this special thing that's between us. Maybe see where it leads us."

Two hours later, back at the arena, Tess saddled Whiskey but was still thinking about Luke. After she'd showered and dressed, he'd dropped her off at the stalls. Then he went back to the ranch to clean up and to check on Bernice and her dad.

She was trying her best not to fall in love with the man, but it was getting damned difficult. Most of her life she'd never depended on anyone besides her dad. But that had slowly changed when Bernice came into the family, and when she finally let the Randells help out. But there had been no one in her life since she'd been involved with Livy's father. Could she let Luke into her life…and risk sharing her feelings with him?

Tess finished checking Whiskey's tack, then they headed toward the arena. She couldn't help but look around, wanting to see a familiar face. But she knew that Bernice had to stay with her father, and her daughter would be tired after the sleepover. She remembered Luke said he'd be back, but would he make it in time?

"Looks like we're on our own, fella," she said to her mount as the walked along the narrow aisle to the arena.

Suddenly she heard her name called and she searched the crowded stands. Again her name was yelled out and she scanned the faces until she finally located Luke waving at her. She smiled and waved back. Then the man next to Luke stood up and waved at her, too.

Dad. Her dad was here. He came to watch her.

She also saw Bernice and Livy, too. She looked back at Luke. He'd done this for her.

A mistake or not, she couldn't stop how she was feeling. The "damned difficult" just turned to damned impossible.

Smooth Whiskey Doc performed to near perfection. He'd scored a seventy-six in the Saturday session. Once she'd finished her part of the competition, Luke brought her father down to congratulate her. His visit was short, as both he and Livy were tired, so Luke drove her family home. He offered to come back and help her, but she refused his offer.

Two hours later she'd loaded up Whiskey and started the thirty-mile drive home. She found she was anxious to see Luke, too. When she pulled up next to the barn, she was tired, but she had Whiskey to take care of. When she walked around to the back of the trailer she discovered Luke was there already opening the ramp.

"Luke…"

"Thought you could use some help." He dropped the ramp but let her go in and bring the stallion out.

The bay was restless and somewhat excitable, but

Tess brought him under control. "I better let him out in the corral for a few hours."

Together they walked the horse to the gate, and Tess took the rope off Whiskey, then let him go. They both watched him for a few minutes in a comfortable silence.

"He did himself proud this weekend," Luke told her. "I guess that means you're on your way."

She shrugged. "It only means something if I decide to travel on the weekends. And the big competition is even more involved. I'm not sure with Dad how I'll be able to handle it." She smiled. "Thanks for bringing him today." Her voice caught. "It meant a lot to me."

"I'm glad. Ray was pretty proud of you." He put an arm around her shoulder. "So am I."

"Thank you."

His silver gaze held hers. "Why don't you go to the house and get some sleep," he suggested. "I know you didn't get much last night." He smiled. "Neither one of us did. Maybe we should take a nap together."

She blushed. "I don't think that's such a good idea. Neither one of will get any rest."

His grin turned downright sexy. "I'm willing to sacrifice." His mouth covered hers, and she lost any argument.

Not that she was going to fight much anyway.

"I call your ten and raise another ten," Luke said the following Friday evening at Chance's house. It was the Randell men's monthly poker game that also included Hank Barrett. Supposedly, he was the champion poker player of the group.

"You sure you want to make that bet, son?" Hank asked.

Hell no, Luke thought, looking down at the spade flush in his hands. This night's gambling had been a bust so far, and this was the best hand he could scrounge up.

He hadn't come to win, though, just to hang out with the cousins. Since Tess had been so busy this week, he hadn't had much to do except relive in his head their night together. Her win was a good thing for her, but had a down side, too. She'd acquired two more horses to train, and had little time for him.

Hank tossed in the needed chips. "I call. Show your stuff."

Luke laid down his flush and watched Hank toss in his two pairs, queens over fours. The cousins hooted with laughter and Chance slapped Luke on the back as he swept up the plastic chips.

"Beginner's luck," Hank murmured with a wink and a smile.

"I think I need another beer," Cade said as he got up from the table. Jared, Wyatt and Dylan followed him into Joy's kitchen, but Chance stayed. "You want another beer?" he asked.

"Thanks, but I have plenty," Luke said.

Chance grinned. "I see your strategy, cuz. Let the others drink enough to cloud their judgment."

Everyone had left at the room except Chance and Hank. The older man was shuffling the cards when he asked, "How is Brady doing?"

Luke shrugged. "He seemed to be doing okay when I called the hospital yesterday. We talked some, but it wasn't much of a conversation."

Chance stretched his arms over his head. "You're still getting used to each other," he said. "I remember when Jarred, Wyatt and Dylan came here. When we learned they were our brothers, it was strained for a long time. But we've managed to become a family.

"I know we haven't kept in touch with you over the years," Chance said as he glanced at Hank. "We had our own things to deal with, although that's not an excuse, we should have hung together. You and Brady are family. Our family."

Those words hit Luke hard and deep. He would have given anything to hear those words years ago. Would have given anything to be part of a family. "After my parents divorced I never wanted to or ever thought I'd come back here."

His cousins' robust voices filtered in from the kitchen but quieted down as they returned to the table.

"Well, you're here now," Hank said. "I believe there's a good reason for you coming back."

Luke wasn't going to lie. "Yeah, it's because I'm broke and have nowhere else to go."

Chance and Hank exchanged a glance before his cousin spoke. "We've all been there. It's hard to lose everything and have to start over again."

Luke stiffened, hating this feeling. "So now you know why I have to sell the ranch." He raised an eyebrow. "Are you interested in buying?"

"Maybe," Chance said. "And maybe we're also interested in investing in it."

"If you say you want me to be a cattle rancher—"

Chance held up a hand. "No, you've made that

clear. What we're interested in is the acreage along Mustang Valley."

Hank spoke up. "I've been protecting that herd of ponies for a lot of years. I want to see it continue after I'm gone. I'm thinking the only way I can do that is by buying the land."

"Whoa, Hank. I'm not even sure what that land is worth." Luke wasn't going to give it away, either. "Besides, I've already been approached about developing that area," he sort of fibbed, knowing Gina's father was lurking in the shadows. So it had to be worth a lot.

Hank nodded. "Developers have been after my section of the valley, too. But we've managed to hold on to it."

Chance spoke up then. "We also know that to protect the mustangs in the valley, there has to be a way to generate income in the family business for the next generations. So we need to make some compromises. That's the reason we need you and Brady to join forces with us."

"And do what?"

"We want to develop the property edging the valley."

Luke tried, but failed to hide his shock. "Sorry, did I hear you right?"

Chance nodded. "Yes, you heard right. But although we want to build on our land, that doesn't mean we want to destroy the landscape. The deal you were involved with in Dallas had to do with gated horse property." He glanced at his brothers. "Would something like that work here?"

Luke's mind was reeling with ideas, also Gina's recent proposition. "Of course it would. You could control how much land is developed, regulate the rules of the gated community. For instance, selling as retirement property, and not letting certain vehicles that harm the environment on the property."

Cade spoke first. "That was the first thing we did when we opened the nature retreat. No cars or trucks."

Luke's enthusiasm was growing. "Then carry that rule throughout the gated property, except on designated roads."

The brothers looked thoughtful, then Chance said, "Would you have a look at our nature retreat?"

Luke wasn't sure he knew what was going on. "First of all, I'd want to know what you have planned. Do you want to buy all the Rocking R?"

Chance shook his head. "Just the section that is across the creek in the valley. That's between Brady, you and Hank. Some acreage from yours and Brady's property, added to the Randells' property that borders the valley will make up the gated community. Of course, we'd like to work out a deal that makes us all partners.

"We could put up most of the capital. We don't have endless funds, so we want you to come up with a idea of what such a project would cost us. And if it's feasible, we would like to hire you as project manager."

A hundred things swarmed in Luke's head. This was like a dream, but soon reality brought things into focus. And were the Randells really just wanting the valley land?

"Hold it. Before we get carried away, I need to think about this. And there's someone who has to give his go-ahead, too. You need Brady to go along."

"The Rocking R has several sections," Chance said. "If Brady decides to give up his military career and wants to ranch, there's enough land so he can raise a small herd and plenty for you, too…to do whatever you want with it."

Immediately Luke thought of Tess's horses. She could stay right here and build her business. Hell, she could even expand. Slow down, he warned himself. Wasn't this how he'd gotten into trouble in Dallas, trusting to easily?

"I'm going to need to talk with Brady, and right now he's not crazy about me being his brother."

Cade stood. "Looks like we'll have to persuade both our cousins that we'll be there for them. That you're part of this family."

CHAPTER NINE

A LITTLE more than a week after the show, Tess walked out of the barn. Thanks to Whiskey's performance, she now had two more horses to train. She'd worked them both, along with her own today, and was exhausted but knew the extra money would help out. She needed to be prepared for when her dad needed more care.

Time was running out for her, too. She wasn't sure what was going on with the Rocking R. She had to be prepared for if or when Luke sold the place.

When she'd let him stay with her the night of the horse show, she'd known the facts of life. There hadn't been any declarations of love from him, or any promises to stay in San Angelo. Still, Tess hadn't been able to resist him. He'd charmed her with kindness and thoughtfulness, not to mention his sex appeal. How could she not fall in love with the man?

She'd been walking around in a daze just waiting for him to return. He'd gone to the hospital in Washington again, trying to convince his brother to sell part of the Rocking R. She wanted to hate him for not loving and cherishing the place the way she did. But deep down she knew he cared more than he let on, and there wasn't any choice for him.

But even worse, Luke was walking away from more than just the land, it was his family. Whether he knew it or not, it was going be hard for him to leave the Randells. She hoped if that day came, he'd be sorry to leave her, too.

Tess made her way past Luke's house and down the gravel road where a yellow school bus had just pulled up. She watched with pride as Livy climbed off and waved at the driver before starting toward her. As much as she hated her daughter being away, Livy loved going to school and all the new friends she'd made. Unlike her mother, the five-year-old was a social butterfly.

Livy spotted her and took off running to her. "Mommy, look at my picture. I got a star." She held up the drawing of a large dark horse.

"Wow, that's great."

"It's Whiskey," her daughter said.

"I can tell by his markings. I'll have to hang this one up, for sure."

Hand in hand they started down the road. "I really wanted to give it to Mr. Luke."

Tess's heart sank. Her daughter was so attached to him. What would happen if he left? "Well, he isn't home yet."

Livy's smile faded. "Is he coming back?"

She nodded. "Remember, he went to see his brother in the hospital."

"I know. He has a broken leg." She glanced up at her mother. "Maybe I should draw him a picture, too."

"That would be nice."

As much as Tess tried to keep her feelings for Luke at bay, he'd managed to sneak into her heart deeper and deeper, even though they hadn't had much time together since the horse show. The day he left for this trip, he pulled her into his arms and gave her a slow, drugging kiss that was filled with promise and hope. By the time he released her, she could barely stand on her own, making her imagine it was possible they could be together. Then two days had passed without a word.

They were just passing the house when a car drove down the road. Luke's BMW. He honked as he pulled into the drive.

Livy jumped up and down. "Mommy, Mr. Luke is home."

Tess couldn't help but smile. "I can see that," she said as Luke climbed out of the car.

He waved and walked toward them. For the first time in a long time, Tess saw a different man. He was dressed in suit trousers and a white shirt with a tie. There was little resemblance of the laid-back cowboy she'd come to know and love.

This man was all about business.

"Hi, Mr. Luke. You're back," Livy cried and she went to him. "I made you a picture 'cause I missed you."

"Hi, shortcake." He hugged the girl. "I missed you, too." He glanced over the picture, "This is great," he said then looked at her. "Hi, Tess."

"Hi, Luke." She felt achy all over, needing to feel his arms around her. "It's good to have you home."

"It's good to be back." He sighed and glanced at his watch.

"Mr. Luke." Livy tugged on his sleeve. "Maybe you can go riding with us. Mommy, can we go?"

"Right now isn't a good time, shortcake," Luke answered. "I have a meeting in a few minutes."

"Oh…" She lowered her head in disappointment.

"We'll make it another day." He knelt down. "Hey, why don't you go hang your picture on my refrigerator? There's tape in the drawer by the phone."

Luke watched Livy until she disappeared into his house. All the way back to the ranch, he'd been dreading talking to Tess. But he owed her an explanation.

"I wanted to walk to you, but I can't now. I've got a meeting with Buck Chilton and Gina."

She looked confused. "Your old business partners?"

He nodded. "Buck has an investment proposition he wants me to look at."

"I thought he was the one who caused you to lose everything before."

He didn't deny it. "I'm just going to listen to what he has to offer. Beside, this time I'd make sure I had control of any project, if we get together."

Her breath caught. "Sounds like you're already decided."

"No, I haven't," he quickly answered. "I have another offer."

"For the ranch? You've had an offer for the Rocking R. Is that what you wanted to talk to me about?"

"The offer is for part of the ranch. And, yes, it's part of the reason." He looked around. "It's hard to explain, Tess, but I also need to hear Chilton out. There are several investors who are interested in reviving my project in Dallas and here at the Rocking R. I'd lost so much before—including my reputation—that I can't just leave things the way they were. Can you understand that?"

"So you'll be moving back to Dallas." The sadness in her eyes tore at him. "Why should I be surprised. Hadn't it been your plan all along?"

He couldn't deny it. "At one time, yes. A lot has happened since then." He still had trouble telling her his biggest fear. "I met you."

A car coming down the drive drew their attention. The luxury vehicle parked at the house, and Gina and Buck climbed out. "Damn. I need to go." He didn't want Gina coming down here.

He looked back at Tess, but she already closed herself off. "Don't let me keep you. You know what they say, Time Is Money."

"It not like that, Tess. But I have to do what's best… for everyone."

"And the hell with your family."

He stiffened. "Just because we have the same last name doesn't make us a family."

It was after ten o'clock when the business meeting finally broke up. Luke was tired when he went to the kitchen and grabbed a beer. He'd been right about Chilton's proposal. It had been for the Mustang Valley property. Yet, even with the valley land off the table, because it was already promised to Hank, Buck wasn't about to give up. What surprised Luke the most had been the number of investors Chilton had been able to round up for this project.

In return all Luke had to do was contribute his and Brady's share of the land that bordered the valley. What wasn't in the deal was the house and outer buildings and enough acreage to run a small herd if Brady retired to live here.

Luke leaned against the counter and took a drink of his beer. His half brother wasn't crazy about him to begin with, but Brady had listened to Chance's pitch about the Randell Corporation's five-year plan. Would he be willing to listen to Luke about a second offer? Either choice they made, he and Brady had a lot to decide. And somehow they had to agree on it together.

That left Luke a lot to think about before he headed back to Washington. Was the intrigue of Buck's deal only because he wanted to rebuild his reputation in the business? Was the reason he hadn't just accepted the Randell deal because he didn't feel he'd fit in here? He thought back to the little boy who'd been devastated when he lost his home and his father.

Could he really be a part of this family again?

Then there was Tess. His decision affected her, too. He cared about her and her family. Even if he chose to return to Dallas, he wouldn't abandon her. Her horse-training business was here in this area. She'd needed a place for Ray, for Livy. He was reasonably sure that Brady wouldn't object to her living in the house, and her using the corral and barn.

So if Luke chose Buck's deal and returned to Dallas, that would remove any guilt he felt about selling part of the ranch. Tess would have her dream and he'd have his.

Isn't that what he'd worked for? Getting back into the game with the big boys.

Luke's attention went to the refrigerator and the picture hanging crookedly on the door. A funny feeling rushed through him thinking about little Livy. He found he'd looked forward to seeing her every day, sharing things with her and her mother. Strange how in only a few weeks he'd let three women and one old man get under his skin. Not to mention a bunch of rowdy cousins.

"Hiding out?"

He looked around to find Gina standing in the doorway.

"I got thirsty." He raised his bottle of beer.

"I hope you're not having second thoughts."

"Believe me, I'm having more than a few. Buck's offered me a great deal once before, and look how that turned out."

"That isn't going to happen again, not with all your demands in writing."

"It's just good business." Luke wasn't fool enough to make any mistakes this time. He'd never lose everything again. But the gamble was even bigger now. There was Brady to think about. His brother's military career was on the line. Luke had learned that pilots who had to eject from their planes had to go in front of a review board to be deemed fit to fly again. For Brady, he still had a long time to go before that happened, if ever.

Gina came across the room. "I have to say, it'll make me happy if you come back to Dallas." She placed her hands on his chest. "I've missed you."

He removed her hands, hoping that she wasn't

offering anything else to sweeten the deal. "It isn't a good idea to mix possible business with pleasure."

"If you're worried about me leaving you again—I won't. I made a big mistake."

He doubted that. If anything, Gina was loyal to herself and maybe her daddy. "I want something different now, Gina. And I'll never work with someone I can't trust."

She glared at him. "It's her, isn't it? That cowgirl."

He wasn't going to give Gina any information about Tess. "This is a business deal, and if I accept it or not, that's all that will be between us." He sighed. "And I believe it's past time to end this meeting."

Her anger was obvious. "I hope you aren't foolish enough to pass up what's right in front of you. Because Daddy is giving you a second chance, and you should take it. So there's only one choice to make." Then she marched out of the room. He heard voices then and the sound of the front door closing.

"If only that were true," he murmured, "life would be so easy." He went to the window and saw the light on in the barn. Tess. He felt his body tighten with need as he recalled their night together. How she felt in his arms. Suddenly he knew. Somehow he needed to find a way back to her.

It was nearly midnight when Tess walked out of the barn, aching with fatigue. She'd groomed Dusty and Lady, cleaned stalls and polished tack, hoping the hard labor would drive everything from her mind and allow her to sleep tonight. Help her forget.

When Tess recognized the shadowy figure coming

toward here, she tensed. No, she didn't want to talk with Luke. Not now.

"Tess," he called as he came into the light. "What are you doing out here so late?"

"I was working."

"You need sleep more."

"I can take care of myself, Luke. So don't worry, I'm headed to bed right now." She tried to move around him, but he reached for her.

"Could you give me a minute, Tess?"

She didn't want to listen anymore. "I've heard it all, Luke. We've talked it to death. And in the end you'll go back to Dallas."

"That hasn't been decided yet." He paused. "But that doesn't change the fact that I care about you." He drew her into his arms and kissed her.

She put up a weak protest, but soon surrendered to the sensations he created, to the need, to the desire. She ached for this man, probably always would, but it didn't mean that was a good thing. Not when he wouldn't be there for her, not when money meant more than family.

She broke off the kiss and stumbled backward. "You have every right to sell the ranch, Luke." She blinked back tears. "But I don't have to like it."

"It's only part of the Rocking R. And remember, I'm not in this alone, I have to give Brady the chance to look over all the offers, too."

"He's going along with your plans to develop the land?"

"He's practical, Tess. We can't afford to keep this place going without generating some income." Luke took a step closer. "Tess, I don't want you to have to leave here. No matter what I decide I'd never let that happen."

Tess's chest tightened. "Would that ease your conscience, Luke? Well, don't worry, I can take care of my family. But the Rocking R is more than a just land, it's been in your family for generations. And selling to the highest bidder doesn't seem right. You might have had issues with your father, but don't give away your heritage."

She brushed away a tear. "You've been given a second chance here. A chance to put down roots, to make a real home. That's got to mean something to you. How can you think about selling it to strangers?"

"Maybe because I don't have a choice." He shrugged. "Maybe what I want is out of my reach."

Tess wanted to argue that fact, but he had to make this decision on his own. If he didn't want her, it was better if she let him go now. She shook her head. "Maybe you aren't reaching far enough for that dream."

His eyes were pleading, then quickly he turned angry. "I stopped dreaming a long time ago. They never came true."

Tears clouded her vision. She knew he was talking about the young boy who left here years ago. "It could this time, Luke. Trust in yourself, in your family. Just don't walk away."

She watched the emotions play across his face. "I'll let you know what's decided about the ranch." His gaze held hers. "Good luck, Tess." He turned and walked off.

Tess hugged herself, the ache in her chest almost unbearable. She had to fight to keep from going after him, knowing in the end if he truly wanted to leave she couldn't stop him. And soon she'd just be a distant memory.

She prayed the same thing would happen for her, that someday she would stop loving Luke. But she knew it was going to take a long time.

Over the next week Luke managed to keep busy. He kept in close touch with the architectural firm that the Randells had hired to draw up tentative plans for the Mustang Valley project, which had been officially named Golden Meadow Estates.

Buck Chilton had been in close touch, also. His architect was due to send him plans by the following week. Luke had flown to Washington to see Brady again, giving him Chilton's offer to go over. He hoped that his brother would be the one to make the final decision, or at least, buy him out of his half of the ranch. Then Luke could go back to his life in Dallas to try to start over.

In his makeshift office in the kitchen, he leaned back in the chair. If the Randell project went ahead, the only thing they'd wanted from Brady or him was the land, and that Luke take the reins as project manager.

And there were always risks in real estate. Thank goodness the Golden Meadows Estates target market was a wealthier clientele. The corporate type who wanted the quiet ranch life without all the work. All they needed was to load up the horse properties' homes and stables with all the right high-end amenities to impress buyers.

Luke rubbed his eyes. His thoughts turned to Tess. Since last week he'd only managed to sneak a glance at her from the bedroom window when she worked in the corral. He'd also spotted her loading Whiskey into the horse trailer. Later he learned she'd gone to another show. Chance had called and asked if he'd wanted to go, but Luke declined. His cousin later reported back that she'd placed well again.

Luke was happy for Tess. He wished he could have shared in her victory, but she didn't want him there. Her rejection hurt more than he'd thought possible.

He glanced out the window when Chance's truck pulled up. Luke put on a smile and let his cousin inside the kitchen.

"Hi, Luke."

"If you're here to bug me about my answer, I still can't give you one."

Chance frowned at him. "That's not why I came by. Besides, it's only good business sense to look for other options." There was a pause, then Chance asked, "Have you heard anything from Brady?"

"No, but you know he didn't want to sell in the first place. That's probably why he's taking his time. He only let go of the valley land because it wouldn't get developed. He keeps talking about how it was our father's dream to come back here."

Chance took off his hat and placed it on the counter. "That's understandable, this ranch has been in the Randell family for generations. Maybe Brady is thinking about the future, too."

He shrugged. "I don't exactly feel the same way."

"I felt like you for a long time after my dad left us. I wanted nothing that was his. I was going get my own place, make a name for myself. I thought I found the perfect piece of land, the old Kirby place. I lucked out when it went up for auction."

Luke walked to the coffeemaker and filled two mugs and handed one to Chance. "Then I went over one day and found Mrs. Kirby's niece there claiming her inheritance. A very pregnant Joy Spencer, and she just happened to be in labor."

Luke took a slow drink from his cup. "What happened?"

"I didn't have much choice," he said. "I delivered Katie, right there in the barn." There was a faraway look in his cousin's eyes. "I fell in love with that little girl and soon after her mother. I learned that Joy was running from her dead husband's parents. They wanted to take the baby away. So Joy asked me to marry her, and in turn she'd sign over parts of the ranch."

"What did you do?"

He smiled. "Well, obviously I married her."

"Did her in-laws ever find her?"

"Yeah, I walked out on her, thinking I wasn't good enough to be a father." He tensed. "You know, my daddy's reputation and I'd tangled with the law in my youth, so I thought I'd hinder Joy's custody chances. Then I realized I wanted to be Joy's husband and Katie's father." He studied Luke for a moment. "At the end of the day, that's all that really matters. How much do you love each other."

Chance studied Luke. "That's why I stopped by, cuz. You've been cooped up here for nearly a week, trying to figure out what's the best business deal to take. This is what my brothers and I would say is 'a gut call.' You can't think about the money, but what's good for you and Brady. And whether you can live with it."

Luke sighed and went to the window. "I didn't think the memories would be so strong. There are some good ones—then Dad left me and Mom."

"I know that feeling, cuz." Chance stared into his mug. "Jack Randell was a piece of work. But I had Hank and my brothers. You were alone to deal with all the crap." He looked at Luke. "I'd like to think this was your daddy's way of giving you a second chance. A chance to meet your brother and your cousins. I have to say, there nothing like family around. That's something that Hank taught us."

Luke's chest was suddenly tight with emotions. He felt raw and exposed, knowing his cousin could read him so easily.

"And just so you know," Chance began. "My brothers and I didn't offer you this deal because you own some Randell land. We offered you the deal because you and Brady are family. And we want to build a future for us and our children."

A lump seemed to lodge in Luke's throat. He couldn't speak.

"I know we're still strangers to you. We hope that will change. If I've learned anything, cuz, it's that family matters."

Before Luke could answer, he was distracted, seeing a man coming up the back steps. Ray Meyers. Luke opened the screen door and invited him inside. "Ray, good to see you again."

The older man blinked. "Sam?"

Luke exchanged a look with Chance. "No, Ray, Sam was my father, he died. Remember, I'm Luke."

Ray frowned. "Oh, I'm sorry to hear about your daddy's passing." He looked around the kitchen. "One time he told me that he was going to come back here… Someday…bringin' his boys home. Oh, he loved his boys. He talked about you all the time. Even showed me a picture." Tears formed in the old man's eyes. "He was plum sorry about what happened…havin' to leave you."

He wanted to believe that Ray's words weren't just gibberish. "Sam told you that?"

Ray's eyes glazed over, and he looked around, confused. "Do you know where my Theresa went? She said she'd come for me…but I waited and waited…"

Luke and Chance exchanged a look. "Well, she's probably busy with the horses. How about I take you to her?" Luke took Ray by the arm and they walked out the back door.

Luke knew at that moment, no matter what, he'd do everything in his power not to ever uproot the Meyerses. It was their home, as much if not more than his. Just as they stepped off the porch, Tess came running from her house, still dressed in her work clothes of jeans and leather chaps. She looked frazzled, but relieved to see her father.

"Dad," she called. There were tears in her eyes as she hurried toward him.

Luke was hungry for the sight of her. Since she'd been avoiding him, he hadn't seen her close up for too long. She looked tired but as beautiful as ever. Her eyes were still mesmerizing, her scent was still intoxicating, her body was still tantalizing.

"Thank you, Luke. I'm sorry he bothered you."

"He's never a bother, Tess. I'm glad he came for a visit." Luke turned to her father. "You come back anytime, Ray. I want you to tell me more about Sam."

The old man looked at his daughter. "Tess, this here is Sam's boy. Did you know that?"

"Yes, Dad, I know that. Now you need to come home. Bernice has your supper ready."

The older man seemed confused, then he smiled. "My little sister?"

Tess tugged on his arm, "Yes, Bernice is your sister."

Just then Livy came running toward the group. "Grandpa, you got found." She hugged him.

"I don't know what the fuss is about, child," Ray said. "I just went to see Sam's boy."

"Well, now we can go and have supper," Tess said, and tugged her father in the direction of the house. But not before Luke caught her glance. The heated stare sizzled between them before she quickly turned away.

Livy hung back, those big blue eyes looking up at him. "Mr. Luke, Mom said you're working really, really hard and we can't bother you. Are you done yet?"

Luke swallowed hard as crouched down in front of her. "I'm never too busy for you, shortcake. You come by anytime you want."

She rewarded him with a smile. "Jinx wants to come, too."

"Sure, the more the merrier."

She hugged him. "Thanks. Bye, Mr. Luke and Mr. Chance."

Livy caught up with her mother and grandfather, and they walked away together. Luke ached to go with them, to help her. To let Tess know she wasn't alone. That he would be there for her. Instead, he could only stand there, in the middle of the yard, and watch the family he'd always wanted walk away.

Chance came up beside him. "Man, that's a lot for Tess to deal with. I'm glad she's got you here."

"She thinks I'm gonna leave her and go back to Dallas."

"So you gonna prove her wrong?" Chance arched an eyebrow. "Or are you just as stubborn as the rest of us, and can't admit that you're crazy about the woman?"

Luke had never realized how much he could want someone. Or how much it would hurt to watch her walk away.

He had to find a way to make things right.

"I've made a lot of mistakes. She really could do better."

Chance gave him a sideways glance. "You might as well think of a way to win her over, because I'm beginning to believe the Randell men only love once. And it's forever."

CHAPTER TEN

TESS was in the corral, having just finished a session with Whiskey. She'd been busy for days working her four boarded horses. The extra money coming in was great, though. It helped pay for her dad's treatment, and she'd been able to hire part-time help.

Brandon Randell came by after his college classes. He didn't even seem to care about the low pay, because she knew he loved working with the horses. And she was happy to have him.

The extra money also enabled her to spend time with Livy after she got home from school. Yet her nights were filled with loneliness. When she did manage to sleep, she dreamed about Luke and how tenderly he'd made love to her. She would wake up, her body aching for him.

Some nights she'd gone out to the porch and looked toward Luke's house. She'd pushed him away so many times. Would he want her if she showed up at his door?

"Tess…"

She swung around to see Brandon. "Oh, I'm sorry, Brandon. Did you need something?"

"I just asked if you wanted me to work the chestnut today."

"Sure. I did a short workout with her this morning," she said. "But I want to take it slow, she's still pretty green."

The eighteen-year-old grinned. "Okay. Oh, Dad wanted me to tell you that he's doing the roundup next weekend. Is it okay if your herd goes at the same time?"

"That sounds great. I'll be there to help out."

Tess walked Whiskey into the barn, finished for the rest of the afternoon. She led the bay stallion into his stall and began to remove the saddle when she saw Luke coming down the aisle with a young girl, a pretty brunette dressed in jeans and a T-shirt. Tess didn't even have time to prepare for the visitors before they arrived at the stall.

"Tess," Luke said. "This is Shelly Greenly. She's looking for Brandon."

She felt relief and didn't know why. "Hello, Shelly. It's nice to meet you."

"It's an honor to meet you, too. Brandon talks about you all the time."

Tess was a little embarrassed with the praise. "Why, thank you. You can catch Brandon in the corral. He's working one of the horses."

"I promise not to disturb him. I just have to ask him something. It will only take a minute." She wandered off and through the double doors.

Tess turned back to Luke, trying to eat up the sight of him. He was dressed in business attire, but had on shiny cowboy boots. She quickly glanced away. "You could have taken her straight to Brandon yourself. You don't have to ask permission."

"I didn't want to disturb anyone while they're working. I thought it best to get the okay from you."

"Bringing Brandon's girlfriend here will disturb him no matter what."

Luke couldn't help but smile. He knew the feeling. Just seeing Tess made him ache. "More than likely," he said, then couldn't seem to come up with any more small talk. "Well, I'd better let you get back to work."

"Actually, I'm about finished. It's been nice to have Brandon here. He gives me more free time."

He paused surprised she was interested in talking to him. "I'm glad. You should take time for yourself." His gaze locked on her mouth, until he had to look away. "How's your dad?"

"Same. He has his good days and bad days." She lifted the saddle off the stallion, and Luke took it from her. She removed the bridle. Together, they walked to the tack room. "His time at the seniors' center is one of the highlights of his week."

"Good. Tell Ray I said hi."

"You can tell him yourself, if you want."

He placed the saddle on the stand, then he pinned her with a stare. "I want a lot of things Tess, but some of them aren't possible right now."

She glanced away. "How is your brother?"

"He's good. He wants out of the hospital, but the doctors want to be sure someone is with him." Luke folded his arms across his chest. He caught a whiff of her, the smell of leather, horses, and her own unique scent. He blinked to bring himself back to reality. "I'm going to see him tomorrow, to try and convince him to come here."

"Oh, Luke, that's wonderful. You two will have a chance to get to know each other."

"Or kill each other."

"Or decide what to do with the ranch," she said.

"I think Brady and I have finally come to terms on that," he said. Thanks to Chance, his cousin made him see clearly what was important. Tess. And he'd been working day and night to get things in place.

"Then you're moving back to Dallas."

He came closer. "You seem awfully eager to send me there. What if I don't want to go? What if I want to hang around?"

He watched her swallow. "That's a decision for you to make."

"A little encouragement would go a long way." And he wanted her to understand that he needed to find his way back. "Why don't you come up to the house tonight? We'll talk about it."

She shook her head. "It's not any of my business. Just tell me if and when you need us to move out."

He was angry now. Everything he'd done was because he cared so much about this woman. "Have I ever asked you to leave? Do you truly think I'd push you and your family out of here?"

"You have Brady to think about now," she told him. "He'll have some say about us being here."

"The hell he will," Luke said as he reached for her and brought her closer. "What do I have to say to get you to believe me, Tess?" he asked, his voice low. "Your family will always have a home here."

He saw the tears in her eyes. "Thank you."

He hung on to the last of his resolve as her luminous eyes locked with his. He'd missed so much.

He wanted to devour her right there, taste her sweetness, feel her strength…her love. But he couldn't. Not until he could offer her a lifetime commitment.

"There's so much I want to tell you," he breathed. "How much you mean to me…" His stomach knotted in frustration. "Right now I need to iron things out with Brady."

She hesitated. "And that's the most important thing."

"My feelings for you don't stop just because I found my brother."

"But your family has to come first, just like my family does. We both have responsibilities, Luke. Right now there isn't time for anything else."

The next afternoon Luke stood across the solarium at the rehab center. Brady sat in the wheelchair, reading over the contracts. Luke had to let his brother make up his mind on his own over the land sale to Hank, and about building the gated community for either the Randells or Buck Chilton. And he did.

Finally Brady looked up and motioned for Luke to come over. "I appreciate you sending a copy of the contracts to my lawyer."

Those dark eyes of his brother's were so like their father's. Sometimes it was hard to look at Brady, knowing he'd gotten something else from Sam Randell.

"It's not a problem. You should be careful when you invest."

Brady glanced down at the papers again. "Did I tell you that Gina Chilton paid me a visit?"

Luke straightened. "No, you didn't. That's even low for her. Did she pressure you to selling?"

He raised an eyebrow. "She makes it hard to turn her down."

Luke could just imagine. "I know. I've see her in action."

Brady shrugged as if he wasn't impressed. "I have to tell you I'm impressed with what this Barrett guy is paying for our strip of Rocking R land. Does it have oil on it or what?"

Luke shook his head. "No. Just something he treasures more. Wild mustangs."

For the first time he saw Brady laugh. It made him think they might just have a chance at this brother thing.

Brady sobered. "So you really think we can make some money on this deal with the Randells?"

"In the long term, I do. Chance and I have gone over this several times. They aren't going to compromise the area by overdevelopment. We're keeping a lot of the integrity of the ranch. And as the contract states, the parcels of land in this deal included equal acreage from three ranches, the Circle B, Cade's Moreau Ranch and the Rocking R. When you get released from here, why don't you come and stay with me? I mean at our ranch, at least to see the project get underway."

Brady looked thoughtful. "It looks like I'll need a place to hang out a while." He held out a hand. "I need a pen."

Luke reached into his pocket and gave Brady a pen, but held his breath as his brother signed several copies.

Brady gave everything to Luke. "This doesn't guarantee we're going to be friends. Just business partners."

They shook hands. "Well, partner, what do you say? Do you want to come to the ranch and take a look at your investment?"

"Maybe, but just so you know, I'm not planning to sit in a rocking chair. And as soon as possible, I'll be back in the cockpit."

Luke saw the determination on his brother's face. "Well, until then, I'm looking forward to getting to know my brother."

"Don't get your hopes up."

Luke gritted his teeth as he walked out. "Well, this is going to be a great partnership," he muttered under his breath. Why was he hoping for more?

"Mr. Luke! Mr. Luke!"

Luke went to the back door and looked through the screen at Livy Meyers standing on his porch. His chest tightened seeing the tiny replica of Tess.

"Hey, shortcake." He opening the screen and she walked inside the kitchen. "How are you today?"

She looked up at him with those big blue eyes. "I'm sad 'cause you never come see us anymore. Are you mad at us?"

He crouched down. "Oh, no, Livy. I could never be mad at you. You're my favorite girl."

"But you don't come to my house anymore. Not since that lady came." She wrinkled her nose. "Are you gonna marry her?"

Where had the child gotten that idea? "No, Gina is just someone I used to know in Dallas."

"She's pretty, but not as pretty as Mommy. I hope you

like her best. Katie said if you like a lady you kiss a lot, like her mommy and daddy do. I saw you kiss Mommy once. Do you like kissing her?"

"Yes I do, very much. Almost as much as I like kissing you." He leaned forward and kissed her cheek.

She giggled, but quickly sobered. "I want you to love my mommy. Sometimes I hear her cryin' at night." Tears filled the girl's eyes. "I don't want Mommy to be sad." The child wrapped her arms around Luke's neck and sobbed.

"Oh, Livy. I don't want you or your mother to be sad, either. I never meant for that to happen. And I've been working hard to make sure your mommy is happy again…and you, too."

She raised her head and swiped at her tears. "What are you gonna do?"

He shook his head. "I can't tell you because it's a secret. But you can help me surprise your mother."

Her eyes widened and she nodded.

"I want to talk to your mom. And right now she isn't taking my phone calls." He'd been calling her since he left the hospital with the signed contract from Brady.

"I know. Aunt Bernie said she should let you say your piece before she makes judgments." She frowned. "What does that mean?"

"It means your mommy should listen before she says no."

"She isn't gonna say no 'cause she loves you."

A sudden dryness in Luke's throat made it impossible for him to swallow. "She told you that?"

Livy shook her head. "No, she said that to Aunt Bernie."

"And I want to tell her that I love her, too. So I need your help." He proceeded to explain his plan to the five-year-old, then wrote out a note that Livy was to give to her mother.

With the sweetest kiss, the girl walked out the door, clutching the envelope like a treasure, but stopped on the steps. She turned and looked up at him.

"I've been wishin' real hard every day to have a daddy like you," she said, then swallowed hard. "Have you been wishin' for a little girl like me?"

Luke's heart pounded in his chest. "With all my heart."

"Mommy, are you going riding to Mustang Valley?" Livy asked as Tess stepped off the porch to head to the barn for her afternoon session.

She stopped. "I have work to do, Livy."

Tess had only managed a few hours with the new mare that had arrived two days ago. Work had been her salvation lately. That was until she'd gotten Luke's note yesterday. Then, why had she put on clean clothes and a little makeup?

Her daughter gripped her kitty in her arms. "But you gotta go riding to see Mr. Luke."

The screen door squeaked as Ray came outside. "You gonna go see Sam's boy?" he called to her.

Tess tried to hide the blush heating her face. Did everyone know her business? "Maybe. He probably wants to talk over some business."

"Please, Mommy." Livy jumped up and down. The kitten had enough and leaped out of her arms. "You gotta go see him."

"It is a mighty pretty day for a ride," her father added as he sat down on the porch swing.

Tess wasn't sure what to do. Luke's message played over in her head. *I need to see you. There are too many things left unsaid between us. Luke.*

Truth was she wanted to see him. Maybe it was for the last time, but she needed to keep her wits about her. She told herself it had to do with her future. "Okay, I'll go, just let Aunt Bernie know where I'm headed."

Smiling, the child took off as Tess looked at her father. "Are you okay?"

He smiled. "Yes, I'm fine. You all take good care of me." He went to her. "Maybe you need someone to take of you."

She forced a smile. "You better not let Bernice hear you say that."

He frowned. "It's time, Tess. It's time to let yourself trust someone."

She glanced away. "I don't do well in that department. I'm happier here with you, Bernice and Livy."

"You have a big heart, my girl. You need to share it with someone like Luke."

She swallowed. "Dad, Luke and I are too different. He has a life somewhere else." She wondered how long before he wanted to return to it.

"Bah, that's nonsense. He no more wants to sell this place than he wants to leave you."

Tess was afraid she couldn't hold a man like Luke. "Dad, he's already sold a parcel of land."

Her father looked confused. "Maybe there's a reason for that, Tess. The Rocking R Ranch has several sections, and since he isn't running a herd, maybe he needs the money."

Ray Meyers's loyalty to the Randells was unwavering. She knew Sam hadn't appreciated all the extra things her father had done to keep the place together.

Livy came running out the door. "Aunt Bernie said it's okay to go, Mommy."

Tess looked at her daughter's sly grin. Something was up, and she wasn't sure she wanted to know what it was.

"Give Luke my best," Ray said.

She waved, hating to leave her father. Today was a good day for him. It had been a long time since they'd had a conversation about anything other than his treatment or Livy. It was almost like he was his old self. Of course he wouldn't be for long and she had to remember that. Just as she wouldn't be the same after Luke left here.

CHAPTER ELEVEN

LUKE paced back and forth along the creek, among a row of trees, waiting for Tess. He'd ridden in from Hank's side of the valley, even borrowed a mount from the Circle B Ranch. Autumn was in the air and he could already see the changing of the season. When he'd first come here it was summer and Texas hot. Now, with the leaves starting to change, he could see the beauty that everyone was in awe of. There was something magical about this place.

He glanced out toward the meadow. The herd was gone, but he didn't worry about their temporary absence, because he knew this was their home…forever. And the strip of the Rocking R land Luke and Brady had sold Hank would be added to the parcel that was known as Mustang Valley. And it would remain untouched. From now on this place belonged to the wild ponies that were here long before people had settled here.

Luke sensed someone watching him, and he turned around to see Tess on Whiskey at the top of the ridge. She sat unmoving in the saddle for what seemed forever. His chest tightened with excitement, just watching her. She was an incredible horsewoman.

Tess started down the rise and he walked to meet her. She was beautiful with her curls unbound. She wore jeans and a blue starched blouse. She'd taken special time with herself…for him.

Her horse nudged his hand in greeting. "I glad you could make it."

"You said you needed to see me." She climbed off Whiskey with ease. So graceful and yet strong around the powerful animals.

Tess suddenly felt awkward about coming here. She glanced toward a blanket that was spread out, along with a backpack, then back to Luke.

He was so devastatingly handsome, and he looked more and more as though he belonged here. But did he really want to? "You said you have something to talk to me about."

He leaned forward, and for a split second she thought he was going to kiss her. Or maybe that was her hope.

"Among other things," he told her, then took her hand. "Why don't we sit down and relax?"

She resisted a little. "I don't have much time."

His clear gray eyes bore into her. "Thirty minutes. You've been avoiding my calls for days, I practically had to kidnap you to get some time with you." He smiled. "If I didn't know better I'd think you were afraid to be alone with me."

"I'm not afraid." She marched to the blanket and sat down, then folded her arms. She could feel herself trembling. "Your note said you wanted to talk."

He strolled over, removed his hat and sat down by the backpack. He took out a bottle of wine. "Chance says

this is a good vintage, and it's from a local vineyard."
Luke had already uncorked the bottle.

"I don't want any wine."

"Why? Don't you drink?"

"Not often, but I just don't want any right now." She
had to keep a clear head.

He studied her for a long time. "You're not—
pregnant?"

She felt the heat rise to her face. "No! Oh, no!"

Luke didn't look relieved as his gaze moved down
to her flat stomach. "It's crazy, but part of me feels a
little disappointed."

Tess glanced away in shock. Why was he doing this
to her? "Luke, please, let's not bring up that night." She
stood and walked off toward the meadow. She felt the
cool breeze against her face, but it didn't help the heat
rushing through her body.

Luke came up behind her. "Tess, I didn't mean to
upset you. If you don't want to talk about that night, I
won't, but I want you to know that I've relived that time
we were together, over and over. It was special to me.
You're special to me."

She couldn't let herself think about their lovemak-
ing. It hurt too much. "Yes, it was special, but it was a
fantasy, Luke. We both knew we had to go back to our
lives, back to what's real."

He turned her around. "It doesn't have to be a fantasy,
Tess. What if I want to make it real?" His head lowered
and his lips touched hers.

Tess sucked in a breath. He took her mouth again, but
this time he didn't pull back. He drew her against his

body, his heat. Unable to resist, she wrapped her hands around his neck and allowed him to deepen the kiss. When he finally released her, she wasn't able to speak, or even think clearly.

Luke took a step back and ran fingers through his hair. He had to slow this down. "Damn, if you aren't getting me sidetracked. I brought you here because I wanted to tell you about what I've been working on."

He watched her back straighten. "Don't bother. I've already heard you sold this strip of land."

"I did, but for a good reason. The money will help finance my upcoming project."

"So this is what you wanted to tell me? That soon there are going to be houses built along this creek? Well, I don't want to hear about it."

Luke couldn't believe that she wouldn't even listen to him. "That's it, you're not going to give me a chance to explain?"

"What can you tell me, Luke?" She waved her arms around. "That the mustangs will remain safe? Most think of them as a nuisance, and once people move in, the ponies will slowly disappear." She glared. "And you could have prevented it."

He was stunned. Of course six months ago he would have sold his soul for the right deal. But he wasn't like that anymore. And it hurt that she didn't know him better. "You think so little of me?"

Before Tess could give him an answer, two riders appeared along the rise. They both watched as Hank and Chance made their way toward them.

Luke went to greet the two. "Hi, Hank, Chance."

"Tess, Luke." Hank pushed his hat back. "Sorry to disturb you, but I got call from a neighbor, Merle Townsend about an injured mustang. He's not sure if it's foul play or just the stallions fighting." He glanced around. "Since the herd isn't here, we'll just ride on toward the mesa."

"I'll go with you," Luke volunteered, knowing his time with Tess was over. Probably for good.

"I can go, too," Tess said. "Oh, but I can't ride Whiskey around the herd. He'd stir up those stallions and might get hurt."

Hank stepped in. "Luke, you go on with Chance. I'll stay and keep Tess company until you get back."

Chance's horse shifted. "Merle said it's the palomino stallion, right?"

Hank nodded. "You should be able to spot the blood on the rump, the left side. I'm worried that some kids are using the ponies for target practice."

Luke returned with his horse, his hat pulled down low hiding his eyes. "Ready."

Chance nodded. "Then let's do it, cuz."

Tess watched as Luke mounted up and rode off without even a glance in her direction.

Once they were out of sight, Hank turned to her. "Sorry, we didn't mean to interrupt your afternoon."

Tess nodded. "I should get back to the house, anyway." She started to leave, realizing that Hank had followed her. The spread blanket and the bottle of wine looked like a private time for lovers.

"Luke went to a lot of trouble to make this special."

He gave her a sideways glance. "It's a shame you have to take off."

Tess wasn't ready to talk about this. "Believe me, it isn't a good idea for me to stay."

"I might be an old man, Tess, but not so old that I don't remember wanting to be with a special girl."

"It was a bad idea to come here." She didn't want to stay. "I don't have time to wait around."

"It's not really my business, but shouldn't you hear the man out before you turn him down flat?"

"I already heard it. Hank," she blurted out. "Luke sold this strip of land."

"I know. And it cost me a pretty penny to buy it."

She froze. "You're the one who bought the land?"

Hank nodded. "Figured it was the only way to protect the mustangs, and so the grandkids will be able to enjoy this place." He nodded toward the blanket. "So they, too, can come here to ride, or if they want to spend time alone with someone special. Everyone benefits. Luke agreed, but he just needed to get the okay from Brady."

Tess's mind was reeling. "What about his project? The gated community he plans to build?"

"Yeah, we're all involved in that. We lucked out when Luke and Brady chose to throw in with us. The first Randell Corporation project will break ground in about a month. Of course, there will be a lot of restrictions to protect this valley, and the houses will be far enough away not to disturb the mustangs.

"And Luke's for that?"

"He's a real powerhouse about getting things done.

He's already got people in place to start when we get the okay."

Hank saw the confusion in Tess's pretty blue eyes. Life had been rough on her, and she didn't trust easily. "I think Luke always wanted to stay here. To make a home, to have family around. When his father deserted him, he didn't have any other siblings to rely on. And his mother was too wrapped up in bitterness to see her son's loneliness."

He watched Tess blink back tears as she looked out at the meadow.

"At least when my boys lost their parents, they had each other," Hank continued. "And me and Ella to help ease the pain, and make them feel safe and loved." He grinned. "They turned out pretty good, if I do say so myself. I couldn't love them any more if they were my own blood.

"I'm beginning to feel the same about Luke. He's a good man, Tess." He took her hands and held tight. "And in your heart I think you already know that."

CHAPTER TWELVE

IT WAS nightfall, and he wasn't back yet.

Tess paced the dining room at Luke's house, occasionally stopping to look out the window. She shouldn't be worried. Hank had called earlier and said they'd managed to rope and bring in the wounded mustang. The cousins were celebrating with Luke over his part in the rescue.

So what was she doing waiting for him to come home? Who was to say he'd want to see her now, anyway? She'd pushed him away so many times, and accused him of God knows what. But after she'd finally looked over the architect's plans for Golden Meadow Estates, she realized this was his dream, his plan for all of them. What he'd been trying to tell her all along.

And she'd never given him a chance.

Now it was her turn. She was going to let Luke know how she felt about everything, and her fears, and her feelings for him.

If he'd just come home.

Hugging herself, Tess paced in front of the table where

candles were lit, giving the room a soft glow. The wine from earlier was opened, the glasses ready for a toast.

Oh, God, it looked as if she was trying to seduce him. She felt herself begin to tremble, along with a desperate need to run. No. If she left now, she might never get the opportunity to tell Luke how she felt. Tess poured herself a glass and took a drink.

"I thought you didn't want a drink," a deep voice said.

Tess swung around to find Luke standing in the doorway. "I…I changed my mind."

Her gaze took him in. Even though the lights were dim, she could see the fatigue on his handsome face. She fought to keep from running to him. "Did you find the mustang?"

He nodded. "The pony had a big gash on its rump, and even after we roped him, he continued to fight us all the way back to the Circle B Ranch. The vet arrived just as I was leaving."

"That's good," she said.

The room grew silent. Tess only heard the rapid pounding of her heart. She was quickly losing her nerve. "Well, I probably should get home." She put her glass down on the table and started to walk out when Luke took hold of her arm.

"Why are you here, Tess?"

She made the mistake of looking at him. He mesmerized her, just as he had on that day he first came here. Oh, God, she loved him so much.

"I brought back the things from our ride." She nodded toward the table. There was also a copy of the design plans he'd taken along to show her. "I hope you don't mind…I went over the plans. They're wonderful, Luke."

He didn't look impressed. "I'm glad you like them."

"I do." She sighed, hurt and disappointed that he didn't seem to care. What did she expect? "I'm sorry I didn't look at them earlier."

Luke couldn't believe Tess was here. At first he'd thought she was a dream. His gaze roamed over her, then rested on her face again. "At least you had a chance now."

She was so beautiful with her hair in soft curls, and dressed in a T-shirt with a blouse over it that tied around her tiny waist and a flowing skirt.

She sighed. "It's late, I really should get home."

He couldn't let her walk away. "Tess, what are you really doing here?" Wrong thing to say. "I mean I didn't think you wanted…"

She swallowed. "I know. I wasn't eager to listen earlier." Her gaze locked onto his. "I came to apologize. I should have let you explain before I jumped to conclusions. And I thought since our picnic got interrupted you could tell me about your plans now."

All the way home, Luke had wondered how he was going to live next door to this woman who didn't want anything to do with him. When he stepped into the house and saw Tess waiting for him…

His chest constricted. "Do you really want to hear about it, Tess? I know how you feel about developing the land. But the truth is, Brady and I have no choice. It's the only way we can keep a part of the ranch."

He watched the emotions play across her face. "I know, Luke. I was wrong not to give you a chance. This time I'll listen, I promise."

Luke lowered his head, so close he could feel her

rapid breathing, inhale her sweet scent. "What if I don't feel like talking right now?"

Her hands touched his jaw. "That's okay, too. I'll just follow your lead."

He bent his head and covered her mouth with a kiss that was long, deep and hungry. He tried to reveal his true feelings to her. How much she meant to him.

Tess wanted him like she'd never wanted another man. By the time he released her, they were both breathless.

"I'm going to live right here on the Rocking R, Tess. I want this to be my home."

"It's where you belong, Luke," she said.

"I know. It took me long enough to realize that. Until I came back, I had no idea." His silver gaze searched her face. "You and your family belong here, too."

She liked the sound of that.

"I have a proposition for you. Once we've built and sold the horse property, how would you feel about being the resident horse trainer?"

Tess tried to hide her disappointment, hoping for something a little more personal. "Sure, as long as I can train and compete with Whiskey."

"It will take six months before anything is completed, so you may be so famous you won't give me the time of day."

"That would never happen." She couldn't take her eyes from his. "You've always believed in me."

"That's because you're talented, Tess. Your way with horses is incredible."

"Thank you." She was beginning to feel uncomfortable. Maybe that was all he wanted from her.

"Thank you, too, for making sure my family can stay on. You'll have to let me know the cost of leasing the barn and corrals."

Tess had to get out of there. She began to back away, but before she could get very far, he reached for her.

"Oh, no you don't, Tess Meyers. You aren't leaving yet. Not until I've said it all." He closed his eyes a moment. "I've worked so hard to find a way to keep all this." He glanced away, then swallowed hard. "Why do you think that is?"

She shrugged. Oh, God, she couldn't breathe.

"You. I'm trying to build a future here. A place for you and your family." He drew in a long breath and released it. "I came here nearly broke. I made some bad choices when I worked in Dallas, and it cost me everything. At least, I thought it was everything. I wasn't a nice man."

He released a breath. "Then I met you and your family, and my cousins. I never had that kind of support or acceptance. You gave me all that and more. I wanted to tell you about the project from the first, but I had to make sure that this deal was the real thing."

"It wouldn't change my feelings for you," she admitted, knowing it was the truth.

"It matters to me. Until the complex is built and sold, it's going to be a little tight financially. But if everything goes as planned, we should be doing pretty well in a few years."

Tears clouded her eyes. She didn't care about the money. "You're going to make it work for yourself… and for Brady."

His eyes narrowed. "That may be, but you're the one

I care the most about. I'm doing this for us and *our* future. I love you, Tess."

This time she gasped. "Oh, Luke. I love you, too. I was so worried that I ruined everything. I should have listened to you."

"You didn't ruin anything." He was grinning when he wrapped her in a tight embrace. Then his mouth came down on hers. She didn't remember much after that as the world melted away and there was only this man.

He broke off the kiss, then leaned his forehead against hers. "Does that mean you're gonna take a chance and marry me?"

Tess linked her hands around his neck. "I happen to think you're a sure deal, Lucas Randell. And if that's a proposal, the answer is, Yes. I'll marry you." She pulled his head down to hers in another heated kiss.

"I won't let you down, Tess," he breathed. "You or Livy. You two are the most important people in my life. I love you both so much."

"I know you won't let us down. I was the one who was afraid to love." She sobered. "I've been running for so long, but I couldn't stop myself when you show up here. I never thought I could love anyone as much as I love you."

Luke hadn't realized how much those words meant to him. His life had been so empty. His mouth found hers in a hungry kiss. He couldn't let her go, and he deepened the kiss until they both needed to take a breath.

"Say it again," he breathed against her ear.

"I love you," she repeated. "Thanks for not giving up on me."

"No worry of that. I'm so crazy about you, I would

have come after you." He hugged her and whispered. "And I wanted a family. You and Livy. I couldn't love that little girl more if she were mine. You think she'd let me adopt her?"

More tears threatened. And Tess could only nod. And he kissed her again and again.

"Oh, boy! Oh, boy!" a tiny voice called out.

Luke broke off the kiss and Tess spun around to see Livy dressed in pajamas standing in the doorway.

"Olivia Meyers. What are you doing here?"

The five-year-old tried to look innocent. "I woke up and got scared, Mommy. You weren't in your bed. So I saw the light on here and thought Mr. Luke would help me find you." She walked to Luke and looked up at him with those big eyes. "Are you really going to be my daddy?"

Luke crouched down to the child's level. "If it's all right with you. I've asked your mother to marry me."

She beamed. "I know 'cause I saw you kissing her. It's just like Katie said. You kissed Mommy 'cause you love her the best."

"Yes, I love her best. But I love you a lot, too." He leaned forward and placed a kiss on Livy's cheek. "I still have to ask you something to make this night perfect. I need you, Olivia Meyers, to say you want me to be your daddy."

The child's eyes rounded, and she glanced up at her mother. With Tess's nod, Livy nodded, too. "I've been hopin' you'd be my daddy someday."

Luke drew the tiny child into an embrace. He swallowed the dryness in his throat and managed to say,

"And I was hoping someday I'd have a little girl just like you." Those tiny arms around his neck were the sweetest feeling he'd ever had. "I love you, Olivia Randell."

She pulled back, her eyes wide. "Oh, boy. I'm gonna be Sarah Ann and Katie's cousin."

Suddenly they heard Bernice's voice and looked toward the doorway to see the older woman. "Oh, my, Livy. What are you doing here?"

The child rushed to her aunt. "Aunt Bernie, Mommy and me are gonna marry Mr. Luke." She giggled. "I mean my daddy. He's gonna 'dopt me."

Bernice grinned. "Well, I'll be. Seems there's been a lot going on tonight." She hugged the child, then looked at her niece. "Congratulations, I'm so happy for everyone."

"Thank you, Bernice," Luke said.

"Daddy, are we gonna live here in your house? And what about Grandpa and Aunt Bernice? Are they in our family, too?"

Bernice gasped. "Land sakes child, you ask far too many questions."

Luke wanted no doubts with any of his new family. He hugged Tess to his side. "We're all moving into this house." He looked at Bernice. "There are a lot of rooms to fill—for everyone in the family. Besides, I'm planning on having Bernie's famous pancakes at least once a week."

"Yippee," Livy cried. "I get my own room." She paused and looked at Luke. "Will there still be enough room for a baby sister?"

This time Tess gasped. "Okay, young lady, I think it's

time for you to head back to bed." She went to her daughter and looked pleadingly at her aunt.

The child relented, kissed everyone goodbye and went out the door. Finally they were alone.

"There's still time to back out," Tess teased. "You're getting quite a family."

"And I'm crazy about every one of them. So I guess I hit the jackpot."

"My dad is going to need extra care."

"And we'll make sure he gets it. If you'd looked over the plans, you might have seen that we added an assisted-care facility."

Her finger trembled as she touched her mouth. "Oh, Luke."

"I never want you to have to put your father someplace far away. He'll be around his family as much as possible. This way he'll always be close by and around the horses he loves."

"Oh, Luke, you're such a sweet man."

"I'm glad you finally noticed." He dipped his head to capture her mouth and let her know his hunger for her.

He finally broke off the kiss. "And right now there're just the two of us," he breathed against her ear. "Maybe we can discuss filling those extra bedrooms with babies."

Tess blushed. "You want children?"

"I want to have a child with you," he stressed. "Just maybe not right away."

"There are so many things we haven't talked about."

"We've already talked about the important things. Love and family."

She smiled. "Maybe we should just enjoy the quiet…
and maybe continue our picnic upstairs?"

He touched her face, trying to believe Tess was his.
"We definitely have a lot to celebrate."

EPILOGUE

LUKE glanced at Tess as they rode their horses over the rise toward the valley. So much had happened in the past two months. They had been married in a quiet ceremony at a small country church with just family present. Ray had been able to walk his daughter down the aisle, with Livy as the flower girl. Their honeymoon had been a short weekend trip to San Antonio, but it hadn't mattered to them, they were alone and together.

"Oh, look, Luke. The mustangs are here."

"I told you." He walked Dusty down the slope, then stopped by a tree and climbed off. He led the horse to water, and Tess by his side.

The meadow's grass was green after the latest rain, but some of the huge trees along the creek had lost leaves with winter coming.

"I know you're not disturbing the valley, but I thought the noise of machinery and vehicles would scare off the ponies."

"We've tried hard not to disturb anything."

Golden Meadow Estates had broken ground, but not without a lot of help and dedication. Luke was fortunate in that he'd been able to talk two of his former employees into relocating and coming to work for him.

Since it was off season at the Mustang Valley Nature Ranch, some cabins were available for his staff. And many of the construction laborers were staying at the Circle B bunkhouse to help save on costs.

"Have you been able to talk Brady into coming out here? Hank could bring him in one of the golf carts."

Luke shook his head. "He's not ready." His brother had arrived a few weeks ago and moved into the now vacant foreman's cottage. That was the closest Brady would allow him. There had been no talk about Sam Randell…all the years in between and why they hadn't met. "Brady told me to just leave him alone."

Tess turned to him. "He's got a lot to think about, Luke. He could lose his career over this injury." He placed her hand on his arm. "He's in therapy, isn't he?"

"Dylan said he's been taking Brenna to the cottage. Seems our family physical therapist isn't accepting any of his guff. So at least he's doing his workouts."

Tess pulled off her hat and brushed her hair back. She hadn't had much of a chance to get to know her brother-in-law. She did know she didn't like him holed up in the cottage all alone.

"Maybe we should move him into our house. He really shouldn't be by himself right now."

Luke shook his head. "No. What he needs is a kick in the butt. He has no idea how lucky he was to survive the accident." Her husband smiled. "Or we could send Livy to spend time with him."

Tess smiled, too. Brady might be a pain to everyone,

but she'd seen how patient he'd been with his new niece. "That might not be such a bad idea."

Luke reached for his wife. "I didn't bring you here to talk about Brady." He kissed her nose. "I brought you here for some alone time." He drew her into his arms, and his mouth came down on hers in a tender kiss that quickly stirred their desire, reminding her of their nearly perfect life.

"Oh, boy, I like how you make a statement," she said, leaning her head against his chest. "I take it you're still happy you married me and inherited a ready-made family."

He pulled back and cupped her face. "I've been alone so long that I can't believe I have all this. You and Livy—" he fought the sudden hoarseness in his voice "—you're my heart."

She blinked back the tears. "And you are mine. I love you."

Luke kissed her again, knowing he'd never get enough of her or her love. He knew now why he'd come back to Mustang Valley. To find what he'd always longed for: to come back home…to have a family.

* * * * *

⬥™ Harlequin® A *Romance* FOR EVERY MOOD™

SUSPENSE & PARANORMAL

Heartstopping stories of intrigue and mystery—
where true love always triumphs.

Harlequin Intrigue®

Breathtaking romantic suspense. Crime
stories that will keep you on the edge of
your seat.

Silhouette® Romantic Suspense

Heart-racing sensuality and the promise
of a sweeping romance set against the
backdrop of suspense.

Harlequin® Nocturne™

Dark and sensual paranormal
romance reads that stretch the
boundaries of conflict and desire,
life and death.

Look for these and many other Harlequin and Silhouette
romance books wherever books are sold, including most
bookstores, supermarkets, drugstores and discount stores.

REQUEST YOUR FREE BOOKS!

2 FREE NOVELS
FROM THE ROMANCE COLLECTION
PLUS 2 FREE GIFTS!